"In t[...]pretty tame these days."

"Maybe you're right," Carter replied, turning to face Zoe.

The moonlight slashed through the courtyard and her eyes glimmered in the half light. She licked her lips and the moment melted into steam and heat.

"I didn't tell you how beautiful you look," he whispered.

"No," she said. "You didn't." Her hands smoothed over her belly.

God, the need to touch her... He'd never in his life felt this way. Compelled.

And before he knew it, before he could stop it, he was leaning down to kiss her. Inches from her mouth, he stopped. "Can I please kiss you?"

Her smile illuminated the darkness. "Yes," she sighed.

He'd never kissed a woman while smiling and it was a hot sweetness. Honey on his lips, fire on his tongue.

"Give us a kiss, Zoe!" yelled the paparazzi. Then the night exploded in flashbulbs. The whirr and click of cameras.

Dear Reader,

I can't believe *The Scandal and Carter O'Neill* is the last of The Notorious O'Neills miniseries. The writing and publication of these three books has stretched over such a singular part of my life. When I came up with the idea I was pregnant with my daughter. While I wrote the first book she was an infant napping next to me on the bed and when this book comes out she'll be two and my son will be in kindergarten! *What?! Where has the time gone?*

This series, which was already so much fun and special to write, has also been very personal. Thank you for picking up this book and for those of you who have written me—it means the world.

I hope you like Carter and Zoe's story. I had such a good time finding exactly the right kind of woman to torture Carter…I mean, make him fall in love. She needed to be zany, courageous, driven and then, come to find out, she had to be pregnant, too!

I have never been one of those writers who believed the characters dictated the stories. They were my creations and I was the boss. But Carter and Zoe would not do what I wanted (remarkably similar to my children). So, once I simply followed my characters' lead, some really interesting things began to happen, and Carter and Zoe have been two of my favorite characters to date. To say nothing of Vanessa…

I hope you enjoy the last of The Notorious O'Neills. Please drop me a line at Molly@molly-okeefe.com. I love to hear from readers!

Happy reading!

Molly O'Keefe

The Scandal and Carter O'Neill
Molly O'Keefe

HARLEQUIN®

TORONTO • NEW YORK • LONDON
AMSTERDAM • PARIS • SYDNEY • HAMBURG
STOCKHOLM • ATHENS • TOKYO • MILAN • MADRID
PRAGUE • WARSAW • BUDAPEST • AUCKLAND

Recycling programs
for this product may
not exist in your area.

ISBN-13: 978-0-373-78408-0

THE SCANDAL AND CARTER O'NEILL

This edition published by arrangement with Harlequin Books S.A.

For questions and comments about the quality of this book
please contact us at Customer_eCare@Harlequin.ca.

® and TM are trademarks of the publisher. Trademarks indicated with ® are registered in the United States Patent and Trademark Office, the Canadian Trade Marks Office and in other countries.

www.eHarlequin.com

Printed in U.S.A.

ABOUT THE AUTHOR

Despite how it may appear in her books, Molly O'Keefe has a wonderful mother. She has no experience with bad mothers and cannot explain why many of the mothers in her books are so awful. Molly never intended for her own mother to get those dirty looks at the grocery store. Molly lives in Toronto, Canada, with her husband and two children.

Books by Molly O'Keefe

HARLEQUIN SUPERROMANCE

1365—FAMILY AT STAKE
1385—HIS BEST FRIEND'S BABY
1392—WHO NEEDS CUPID?
          "A Valentine for Rebecca"
1432—UNDERCOVER PROTECTOR
1460—BABY MAKES THREE*
1486—A MAN WORTH KEEPING*
1510—WORTH FIGHTING FOR*
1534—THE SON BETWEEN THEM
1542—THE STORY BETWEEN THEM
1651—THE TEMPTATION OF SAVANNAH O'NEILL**
1657—TYLER O'NEILL'S REDEMPTION**

*The Mitchells of Riverview Inn
**The Notorious O'Neills

For Sarah, Cam, Robert and Katie-Bear.

Thank you for the Friday night dinners,
the Sunday morning skating lessons,
the Springsteen dance parties and for teaching
my son the "pull my finger" joke.

We couldn't ask for better friends.

CHAPTER ONE

THERE WERE TWO KINDS of people in Carter O'Neill's world. Logical people who saw reason and agreed with him about the Jimmie Simpson Community Center. Then there were *the others.* The others, who wanted his blood. Who wanted to string him up by his neck and shove bamboo under his fingernails, just to hear him scream.

Right now, he was surrounded by the others.

Looking out at the mob of seniors and single moms, all he saw was bloodlust in their eyes. Even the toddlers were sharpening their incisors on their teething rings.

But no one looked more furious than Tootie Vogler, who showed up at every single informational meeting, with her Sunday hat and her white gloves and so much anger in her eighty-year-old body she nearly levitated.

"Mrs. Vogler," Carter said with as much calm as he could muster, which couldn't have been much because she bristled, her white curls practically going straight. "Mrs. Vogler, hear me out. As I've explained, the activities and services that are currently offered here will be held in the new building."

"But," she said, standing in the front row of the small gathering being held in the decaying belly of the Jimmie Simpson Community Center, "what happens while you're building that new building?"

It took every muscle in his body to stop himself from rolling his eyes.

"Yeah," one of the mothers said, jiggling a baby in her arms while her toddler ran amuck in the corner, grabbing the cookies they'd laid out. Seriously, she needed to be watching that kid instead of asking the same damn questions he'd heard—and answered—a thousand times already. "How long is it going to take?"

"Once we tear down the existing building it will take a year—"

"A year!" Another one of the mothers cried as if he'd just said he wanted to eat her kid for lunch.

"Well," Mrs. Vogler said, "that's what you say now, but what about what happened over at the Glenview Community Center?"

There were rumbles of agreement, and frankly, the others weren't wrong. The Glenview sat, half-built, a total waste of time and money. There was simply no way the city could finish that project with the limited tax money they had while the existing community centers were in such terrible shape. Never mind the fact that Jimmie Simpson was in low-income Beauregard Town where the programs offered by the center were at capacity and Glenview was over in up-and-coming Spanish Town, where there wasn't nearly the demand for day care and after-school programs.

He'd tried to explain this, but the message was never received and frankly, Carter was feeling like a broken record. A broken record speaking Swahili.

The Glenview Community Center was this administration's albatross. And, since Carter wanted to be voted in when the current mayor's term was up next year, it was his giant hole-in-the-ground cross to bear. "As I've explained numerous times," he said, "that project was spearheaded by a previous administration. And while it's not currently a priority, we are looking into ways to complete the job."

What he couldn't say, though everyone knew it to some degree, was that the previous administration had been so dirty, so backhanded and money hungry, that he still spent half his days trying to make right the terrible wrongs that the former mayor and his staff had perpetrated on this city. But Carter couldn't say that. Nope, diplomacy was his task.

"Well, why doesn't your administration go fix

that mess and leave this community center be?" Mrs. Vogler said, rallying the troops behind her.

"Mrs. Vogler—may I call you Tootie?"

"No."

His composure started to snap and fray.

"Fine. Mrs. Vogler, we *can't* leave this community center alone because this community center is falling down," he cried, pointing to the chipped paint and flickering lightbulbs.

"So," Tootie said. "Fix what's wrong. We're not arguing that nothing needs to be done around here, but why are you tearing the whole thing down?"

"*Everything* needs to be redone here. Plumbing, electrical, a new roof, a new pool. Part of the foundation was damaged during the storms six years ago and I'm telling you the truth—it will cost more to fix Jimmie Simpson, in the long run, than it will cost to rebuild it. I know your lives will be disrupted—"

"I count on the day care here, Mr. O'Neill," one of the mothers said, steely-eyed and angry. He'd blown it again. This wasn't even part of his official job as mayor pro tempore, or president of City Council. He'd taken it on at the mayor's behest, since the totally deserted and decimated Office of Neighborhoods and the overworked Parks and Rec department couldn't do it. But now he was regretting it; he'd had more trouble with the public than any one man could handle.

"Look," he said, inwardly sighing and trying to start fresh. Again. "I've started this off on the wrong foot."

"I'd say," Mrs. Vogler muttered, and he gritted his teeth.

"The parks and recreation department," *who should be handling this mess,* he thought but didn't say, "are working to move your programs to other centers in the city."

"I don't have a car, Mr. O'Neill," a woman said. "It just won't work!"

"For you," he said and then winced as everyone sucked in a scandalized breath. *Backtrack, Carter. Backtrack.* "This is going to be better for this neighborhood in the long run—"

"And what would you know about Beauregard?" another woman asked, who he couldn't see. She was short and in the back, but he caught a glimpse of black hair and pointy features. She looked like an elf.

Great. He even had elves after him.

Honestly, he wanted to go back to his office and get to work on the budget. Or poke himself in the eye with a pencil. Anything would be better than this.

"Are there any more questions?" he asked, admitting defeat. "About things that haven't already been covered?"

"Yeah." A young man, partially hidden behind

Mrs. Vogler, stood and revealed himself. Blood instantly boiled behind Carter's eyes.

All he needed today was this.

"No press," he told Jim Blackwell, who, for a month, had been chasing him from function to function like a hound after a fox. And there wasn't much farther Carter could run.

"I'm just a concerned citizen, Deputy Mayor," Jim said. Smarmy bastard. Carter's title wasn't Deputy Mayor; there wasn't even a deputy mayor position in this city. But when Carter took over the neighborhood issue task force, the *Gazette* had run a political cartoon of him on the front page with a ten-gallon hat, shotgun and a deputy star. In the background, the mayor, as sheriff, snored at his desk.

The deputy part of the joke had stuck.

"Are you aware your father's arraignment has been postponed?" Jim asked.

The question drew whispers and gasps from the women in the crowd.

"I do not discuss my family with the press," he finally said, trying to keep what was left of his dignity in front of the suddenly wide-eyed crowd. He'd worked long and hard to put the Notorious O'Neills behind him, but his father's arrest last month had stirred up all the old rumors.

"I have a question." It was the elf again, waving

her arm in the back row, but Jim talked right over her.

"Last month, your father was arrested in possession of The Pacific Diamond, which was initially part of the Ancient Treasures exhibit stolen from the Bellagio seven years ago. The Pacific Diamond, Ruby and Emerald were all taken." Jim flipped his notes, putting on a heck of a show for the spellbound public. "One man was arrested at that time, a…Joel Woods, who had the emerald in his pocket. He served seven years, claiming all along that he'd worked alone."

"What is your point, Mr. Blackwell?" Carter asked, biting every word.

"Well—" Jim smiled, looking around at the crowd he held in the palm of his hand "—this is interesting, though slightly off topic, but Joel Woods's son is now dating your sister? Is that right?"

Carter didn't say anything.

"Right, sorry, off topic. Back to your father. According to the D.A., they're postponing the arraignment in order to reexamine your father's involvement with the original theft. Both your parents were questioned during the initial investigation."

"Excuse me?" elf girl was saying, but Carter held up a hand, putting her off. Rude, he knew, but he had a fire to put out. A city-politics mosquito to slap down.

"Whatever my father has or has not done, I'm sure will be handled by the appropriate authorities. I have no contact with him."

"What about your mother?"

"My mother?" he asked, startled by the question.

Don't tell me she's gone and gotten arrested, too.

"I haven't seen her in years."

"Would you say…ten?" Jim asked, consulting his notebook, and suddenly the room spun. Carter was dizzy. Sick.

There is no way he could know, he told himself. *No way.*

"Am I right?" Jim asked. "You would have seen her when you testified on her behalf in court ten years ago." Jim held out his tape recorder, his bland face crowned with conceit.

Jim had made a career of shining a light into the dark corners of the previous administration, but for the last two-and-a-half years, Jim Blackwell had been stymied in his efforts to pull up any dirt on the current administration.

But Carter's father's arrest was changing all that.

"You've already done this story, Mr. Blackwell," Carter said. "When my father was arrested, you took great care in giving the residents of Baton Rouge a good look at my bloodline. And I say now what I said then—I am not my family. I have very little contact with my family. I do not discuss them. I think you're repeating yourself," he said.

"I'm just trying to get my time line straight. You testified on your mother's behalf in a breaking and entering case ten years ago. You seem a bit fuzzy on the specifics, which makes me wonder what else you're fuzzy on. There is, after all, a thirty-carat ruby still on the loose."

"We're done here," he said stacking his cards, getting ready to leave. Amanda, his assistant and soon-to-be campaign manager, swung up on his left.

"Answer the damn questions," she breathed in his ear. "Or it looks like you have something to hide."

And then she swung away.

Nausea rolled through him. He did have something to hide. He had a whole family tree of criminals and rogues that needed burying. But Carter gritted his teeth, and stayed. "Yes, it has been ten years since I've seen my mother. We are not in contact. And I have no idea where the ruby is."

"You were her alibi in the breaking and entering case," Jim said. "The charges against her were dismissed on the basis of your testimony," Jim said.

"What is your question?" he asked, knowing in his stomach what the question was going to be.

"No question," Jim said, and Carter nearly sighed in relief. "Just getting my facts straight."

So you can come at me later. Carter had no illusions that Jim Blackwell was just here to get his facts straight. Jim Blackwell was throwing down a gauntlet, right here in front of him, Mrs. Vogler, and the kid with a mouthful of chocolate-chip cookies in the back.

His nausea vanished and he was suddenly clear-headed, sharp-eyed. Jim Blackwell was starting a fight, and Carter loved a fight.

"I feel it's necessary to remind you of my law degree from Old Miss," Carter said. "I understand the legalities of libel better than the previous administration, and I would say after your last article about my family, you are skating on thin ice."

"Is that a threat, Mr. O'Neill?"

"Just helping you get your facts straight, Mr. Blackwell." He glanced over at Amanda, whose smile was sharp, approving. Apparently he'd handled that right. Score one for the Notorious O'Neills.

"We're done here," Carter said and stepped away from the podium toward Amanda, who had pulled out her BlackBerry and was, no doubt, already on damage control.

"Your father is giving me heartburn," she muttered, shooting him one poisonous look. "And now I've got to look out for your mother?"

"No one has any idea where my mother is," he said. "She's a nonissue."

"Excuse me!" a woman cried, and he knew, just *knew* it was elf girl, and he just wasn't up for more questions about how these women would live their lives without this community center.

It was bad politics, he knew that, but he pretended not to hear her.

"Wait a second!" she yelled, her voice sharper. Carter reluctantly turned.

The elf had gotten on a chair. Great.

She was lovely, actually. Her long, shapeless coat had some kind of wild embroidery on it, and her short, ink-black hair sparkled in the light coming through the dirty windows.

A pixie.

She slowly pushed back her long coat to reveal the swell of a very pregnant belly.

Maybe it was the way this day had been going; maybe it was the bloodthirsty toddlers, but some warning system in Carter's head went: uh-oh.

"Where have you been for the last five months?" the elf asked, her eyes snapping. Her hands cupped her belly, and Mrs. Vogler sat down like a stone.

"Oh," she sighed. "You're a bad, bad man."

The whispers started immediately, and the only thought buzzing through Carter's suddenly decimated brain was, thank God there were no cameras.

Jim Blackwell lifted his cell phone and snapped a shot of the pregnant elf on the chair.

"Oh, crap," Amanda said.

"I've never seen this woman in my life," he said to Amanda and to the crowd.

Elf girl shook her head and got off the chair. "I knew you'd say that," she whispered, convincingly heartbroken.

Thank God, the little liar started to walk away.

"You need to go after her," Amanda said, furiously whispering in his ear.

"Are you nuts?"

Amanda pointed to Jim Blackwell, who was writing everything down. "Get to the bottom of it, before he does," she said. "We can't let that guy get the drop on us any more than he has."

Amanda was right. He pushed his notes into her hand, and she immediately stepped forward and began spinning the situation, but it was like waving a tissue in front of a bull. Carter felt every eye, especially Jim Blackwell's, on his back as he approached the girl.

He caught up with her at the front door and put one hand under her elbow. Carefully, so it didn't look as if he was manhandling her, he spun her around and led her back around toward the pool, and the second exit onto an alley, where things would be less busy.

"I'm sorry," she said right away, her voice breathy. "Really, really sorry. I didn't know what else to do."

"About what?" he snapped. "Ruining my career?"

"Getting your attention."

"Really? Nothing but accusing a total stranger of leaving you knocked up and alone?"

"You just kept ignoring me. Which, may I say, was pretty rude."

"Don't talk," he said. "Don't say one more word."

"Okay," she said quickly. "Right. I'll shut up." The silence lasted for all of ten seconds, in which Carter recognized the delicious smell coming off the woman. Ginger cookies. Weird. "Hey, sorry, I know I'm supposed to keep quiet, but could you just ease up on the grip?" she muttered. "And slow down—you're like ten feet taller than me."

It was true. She barely came up to his shoulder and Carter realized he was practically dragging the woman. He didn't even want to imagine what kind of headline that would create, so he slowed down.

He even managed to wave at Mrs. Vogler as if this were all normal, all part of the plan, but she wasn't buying it—she watched, slack-jawed.

He punched open the door to the pool and led her into the giant cavern. As soon as the door shut he dropped her arm, still walking toward the side door onto the alley. Trying to control his suddenly rampaging anger.

"This place really is in bad shape," she said, staring into the empty tiled hole that used to be a pool. "You sure it's going to cost less to rebuild? That seems counterintuitive."

He turned back and looked at her, the pregnant pixie who might have just created the worst scandal to hit this administration, and she was gazing into the deep end.

She must have caught a whiff of his fury because she straightened and managed to look like a very contrite pregnant pixie. Her hands fiddled with the edges of her coat. "I'm sorry," she said, waving her hand behind her. "About all that."

"Why the hell did you lie?" he asked. "Do you even know what you've done?"

"It's complicated."

"Try to explain it," he breathed, barely keeping it together.

"Let's go outside," she said, stepping by him. She gave him a wide, nervous berth, but he still smelled ginger and sugar. Sweet and spicy.

He hit the doors under the unlit and cracked exit sign and led her into the bright warmth of midday. He yanked at his tie.

"Is this a medical situation?" he asked. "Are you off your medication, or escaped from the psych ward?"

The woman was silent, scanning the alley as if searching for someone.

"Do I need to call the cops?" he asked, and that got her attention.

"No," she said quickly. "No cops. I was told—" She blinked big green eyes, and then shut up.

"Told what? By who?" he asked, his voice hard.

"Whom," she whispered.

"I'm sorry?"

"By…ah…whom? It's an object-subject…" She blinked again, the pretty green eyes like pine trees in sunlight. "I'll shut up."

He stepped up to her and looked down at her glossy black hair. "Unless you give me one reasonable answer right now, there will be cops and you will be in more trouble than you can possibly handle."

"A woman gave me a thousand dollars to get you out here alone," she blurted.

Carter blinked, speechless.

"But I don't know where she is." Pixie looked around again.

"What woman?" he finally asked.

"I don't know her name," she said. "She was blond. Pretty."

Carter stepped back. *No,* he thought. *This can't be happening.*

Amanda came barreling out the door they'd just come through.

"What the hell is going on?" she asked.

"Take her," Carter said, gesturing toward the pregnant woman. He didn't even know her name, which was crazy considering the story she'd just started. "Put her in my car and don't let her leave."

"You can't do that," she said, her little face all screwed up with outrage.

He leaned in, close enough to see the freckles across her nose, the thickness of her black eyelashes. "You can wait for me in my car or you can wait for the cops in my car, it's your call."

She took her full bottom lip between her teeth, biting until the pink went white. "Fine," she said, and whirled, her pretty coat sweeping out behind her.

"Who is she?" Amanda asked.

"I have no idea," he said. "But don't let her leave."

Amanda followed the woman through the gray doors, and Carter was left alone in the alleyway.

He stared up at the clouds stretched thin across the slice of blue sky between the buildings. All he ever wanted was to do the right thing. Something good. And somehow it always got screwed up.

"Hello, Carter," a voice behind him said. A voice so familiar, despite its ten-year absence from his life, it made something small and forgotten inside him twist in fear and love. He didn't even have to turn to see her, the perfect blond hair, the thin body no doubt impeccably dressed, the cold, ice pick eyes.

Of course, he thought, she would show up now.

"Hello, Mother," he said.

CHAPTER TWO

ZOE MADISON HAD MADE a lot of mistakes in her life. Big ones, small ones, forest-fire-size ones that had burned her life to the ground.

If there were an authority on mistakes, she was it.

And she knew—from the backseat of Carter O'Neill's expensive car, with its leather seats and fake wood—she knew that what she'd just done, the lie and the drama of it all, was not a mistake.

First of all, Carter O'Neill was going to be fine. A guy like that was born fine. He was simply too good-looking, too cool and calm, to not be fine. He was like James Bond or something. Though, she thought with a smile, James Bond *had* gotten batted around like a cat toy by that wily Tootie Vogler.

He was actually far more handsome when he was frazzled, which was saying something, because it wasn't like the guy was ever hard to look at.

That little scene she'd caused in there would simply blow over.

And if she felt any doubt, any little wormhole of guilt, it was because of the reporter-guy asking the questions. She hadn't counted on a reporter, and that might take some repair work. Maybe she'd write a letter to the editor or something, tell the whole world she was off her meds. Or stalking the handsome deputy mayor with the lips so perfect they should be bronzed.

More likely, though, she'd just be explained away in some kind of press release issued by the mayor's office.

Yeah, she nodded, liking that one the best. They'd take care of it.

The second reason that what she'd done was not a mistake was that the guy was planning on tearing down the heart of this community as if it was nothing; as if a year without day care and senior bingo nights or after-school dance programs was all just an afterthought. A footnote on some memo.

Beauregard had clawed its way out of the gutters and the programs offered at Jimmie Simpson had been part of that. She was part of that. And pretty damn proud.

And third, and most important, she had a thousand dollars in her pocket. Like a roll of hope, heavy and dense. She tucked her hand in her pocket, just to feel the thickness, the tension in the rubber band.

A thousand dollars.

She had no insurance, and her savings were going to be eaten up by the hospital birth, so a thousand dollars could buy a lot of diapers. A little bit of security.

And for that—she put a hand under her belly, where she could feel her little guppy doing a soft-shoe number—she would cause any number of scenes.

For the baby, she'd do anything.

The woman, Amanda, stood outside Zoe's door, with a cell phone attached to her ear, a distracted guard.

Zoe rubbed her hands over the smooth leather and the slick wood panel on the door. Was it real, that wood? Who knew, but fake or real wood in a car was weird. Seriously, did the world need such a thing?

Yeah, she thought, sliding over to the other side of the car, her mind made up. She didn't need to feel bad. Carter would be fine. Money made a lot of things go away, and Carter had money. He had money and shine and polish. Hell, he had a staff.

Watching Amanda's back, she silently opened the door and slowly crept out of the car. Amanda didn't even twitch.

Zoe ran off into the side streets.

"I SHOULD HAVE KNOWN Dad getting arrested would make you surface. What are you doing,

Mom?" Carter asked, dimly wondering why he still called her Mom. After all she'd done, the years of screwing with their lives, he still couldn't just call her Vanessa. It was a little sick.

"Let me see you, Carter," his mother said, her voice gruff with the appropriate amount of manufactured emotion.

He turned, thinking he was prepared, but he wasn't. Could never be. Her presence was a punch in the gut and a slap in the face. A pain and an offense all at the same time. She was lovely, of course. Looking at her, shrouded in cool elegance, you'd never guess she was one step up from being a grifter. A common thief.

Despite her presence in a dirty Baton Rouge alleyway, she looked like Princess Grace.

She looked, actually exactly like Carter's sister, Savannah.

Her smile, a sharp little slash in her face, was like opening a door to a burning room, and he was suddenly filled with anger and fury. Smoke and fire.

"I can't come see—"

"No," he said quickly. "You can't. That was our deal. I testified and you were supposed to stay away from me. From all of us." He stepped toward her, gratified when she flinched, one foot sliding backward.

That's right, he thought, something primal roaring to life, *you'd better be scared of me.*

But then she stopped herself, stiffening her thin shoulders as if facing a firing squad. "You're my son," she said.

He paused and barked out a bitter laugh.

"I understand you're mad, Carter, but there are things we need to talk about."

"Sure there are," he said. "Like why you broke into Savannah's house a few months ago. Twice. That broke our deal, too, *Mom.*" He sneered the last word, because one shouldn't have dirty deals with their mothers, bargains made to keep the distance between them permanent. "You're supposed to stay away from all of us. I should send you to jail."

She blinked the beautiful blue eyes that he and both his siblings had inherited. In the past few years it had gotten so bad he could barely look at Tyler and Savannah and not see his mother. Not see all the ways he'd failed his siblings. The ways he'd let them down.

"We need to talk about the ruby," she said.

"You want to talk about where you hid it, after you stole those gems seven years ago?"

"I didn't steal the gems," she said.

"Dad may go to jail, but I know somehow, you're at the bottom of this. So take your story somewhere else. I'm not buying."

He had a pregnant liar to deal with. A public image that was going to take the beating of a lifetime if Jim Blackwell had his way.

"It's not a story, Carter. I just…is it so wrong to want to see you? To want someone in this family to know the truth?"

It had been twenty years since Vanessa had dropped him, along with his brother, Tyler and sister, Savannah, off with their grandmother, Margot. Ten years since she'd resurfaced to bribe him into lying for her on the stand. And now, suddenly, she thought she deserved a chance to tell her side of the story?

"This family wouldn't know the truth if we sat on it," he snapped. He turned to leave, walking up the slight hill toward the end of the alley.

"I didn't steal the gems and I didn't plant them in the house. You're right. I was looking for them months ago, but I didn't find them. But now that the diamond has surfaced, everyone is going to come looking for that ruby and it could get ugly. For all of us. If they're not at The Manor, there's a chance Margot has them on her."

"Margot?"

"She could be in danger, Carter."

"I can't believe this," Carter sighed. "You're trying to convince me you care? About us? Or someone else getting their hands on the ruby."

"Do you think I would be here if I wasn't worried? If I wasn't serious?"

"Yes."

She sighed, exasperated. "I paid that girl a thousand dollars, Carter."

Right. Money. Not something Mom parted ways with easily.

Vanessa opened her mouth, but from the end of the alley, he heard Jim Blackwell's voice talking to Amanda.

"I don't know where he is," Amanda was saying, very loud.

"You know," Jim said, "for a PR gal, you're a shit liar."

"Monday night," he said to Vanessa, resigning himself to the fact that he needed to manage his family, because out of his control, they could ruin everything. "At 8 p.m., outside of my office. Anyone asks who you are, you lie."

She nodded and stepped into the shadows, the faint click of her heels against the asphalt fading away as Jim Blackwell appeared at the top of the alley.

"I never pegged you as the deadbeat daddy type," Jim said, his face awash with victory. "Not very nice of you."

Carter stalked up the alley, wishing, truly wishing that politics weren't so important to him so that he could just haul off and punch Jim in his fat mouth. But his job, the work he did, the work he wanted to do, it all mattered.

"No comment," was all he said as he stomped by. "And I'll have your job if even one word of this is blown out of proportion."

"Come on, now, Carter. I'm a newsman, I only want to tell the truth. I just don't understand why you have such a problem telling it."

Carter ignored him and continued to his car, where a very stressed Amanda stood.

"What?" he barked, trying to look past her for a glimpse of the lying pregnant elf. The backseat was empty. "Amanda?"

"She's gone," Amanda said. "The girl. She just vanished."

"THIS REALLY HAPPENED?" Tom Gilbert asked, coming to perch his skinny butt on the corner of Jim's desk. Tom was to the City Desk what lunch ladies were to playground bullies—ineffective and overzealous. In a word, useless.

"Of course it happened," Jim said, not looking up from his five hundred words about Carter O'Neill's testimony for his mother ten years ago.

He'd already handed in his story about Carter O'Neill's love child.

Honestly, this might be one of the best days of Jim's life.

"Jim?"

"You've got a picture," Jim said, rolling away from the keyboard to face his boss. "It happened. I've got two old ladies saying they had no idea Zoe Madison was having a thing with the mayor pro tem. What more do you want?"

"News," Tom said, smacking the copy against his knee.

"Carter O'Neill, who is going to announce his candidacy for mayor any minute, knocks a girl up and walks away?" Jim laughed. "That's not news?"

"I don't think it's true," Tom said and Jim sat up.

"You accusing me of lying?"

"No, Jim," Tom sighed. "Christ, you're so defensive I can barely talk to you. What I'm saying is I don't think it's a story. The Mayor Pro Tem office is going to issue a statement saying O'Neill's never even heard of this girl, and I don't want to have to print a retraction in two days for a story tomorrow."

"That might not happen, Tom." *You lily-livered, soft-handed coward,* he thought. "And right now, you've got a public official involved in some pretty crummy stuff. I know it's been awhile since you were out there, but that is news. The girl's broke—a dance teacher or something—she has no insurance, and she just accused Golden Boy Carter O'Neill of knocking her up. It's gonna be all over the region, it's so good."

Tom stood up, his freaking king-of-the-world attitude putting a few more inches on his lollipop build. "Your hard-on for this guy is getting in the way of your judgment. You did good work two years ago on the Marcuzzi administration. No one can take that away from you—"

Especially you, you little nosebleed, Jim thought.

"But not every public official is out to ruin this town."

"Carter O'Neill's father was arrested with a thirty-carat stolen gem! His sister is dating the son of the man arrested for the original theft. The man comes from a family of crooks. His grandmother was a high-paid whore—"

Tom winced, because he had the stomach of a little girl.

"His mother is a known criminal—"

"Convicted once of grand theft auto." Tom shook his head. "You did this story when Richard Bonavie was originally arrested and Carter answered every one of your questions. He has very little contact with his family. Not everyone running this town is dirty. I think the Marcuzzi administration ruined you, made you see crooks were there aren't any."

"Gem theft!" Jim cried. "If Carter has anything to do with it, he's dirtier than Marcuzzi."

"I'm not against you," Tom whispered. "I want to help you. But you're young and fairly new to the city—you keep running around here half-cocked and we're all gonna get burned. There's a difference between journalism and a witch hunt."

"What about the love child story?" Jim asked, ignoring Tom's little pep talk.

Tom sighed. "It runs. Copy already came up with a killer headline," he said and Jim fought back a smile. Of course it would run. It was top-shelf scandal, and scandal sold papers.

"What else are you working on?" Tom asked.

"I've got five hundred words on O'Neill testifying for his mother in a criminal case ten years ago."

"Are you kidding?" Tom asked. "You're turning into a one-trick pony here, Jim."

"You've got a hole on page three," he said with a shrug. "I can fill it."

"Damn," Tom sighed. "Okay, Jim, but let's remember what we're here to do. Tell news, not stories."

CARTER DIDN'T WAIT for the emergency Saturday-morning meeting to officially begin. He stormed into Amanda's office and caught her shoving the last of a doughnut into her mouth.

"What are we going to do?" he asked.

"Knock?" she asked, around a mouthful. "Learn some manners?"

He sighed and slapped the *Gazette* on her desk. The picture of the pregnant elf on that chair stared up at him, mocking him. Jim Blackwell had found out the woman's name—Zoe Madison. It was right there in the caption, and Carter had spent most of the morning finding out what he could about her.

Her address on a scrap of paper burned in his pocket, and he wanted nothing more than to go over to Beauregard Town and strangle her. Of course, that wouldn't do much for his image. Maybe he'd be better off parading her around town and making her tell every single person they met that she'd lied about him.

"He's calling me Deputy Deadbeat Daddy," Carter said through gritted teeth.

"Actually," Amanda said, swallowing and standing, as she gathered a stack of papers in her arms, "so are the *Houston Chronicle,* and the *New Orleans Sentinel* and—" She tossed the papers on the desk, each one hitting the mahogany with a flat thud like a nail in Carter O'Neill's coffin. "The real kicker, the pièce de résistance, if you will—"

"Amanda. We don't need any more theater."

"Third page in *USA Today*. They're all calling you Deputy Deadbeat Daddy."

He hissed as if burned. And it felt that way; his anger was so hot he had to stand up and walk to the window, looking down on St. Louis Street, quiet and slick with rain.

This was going to be his legacy. He could clean up every neighborhood in this city, but he'd still go to his grave as Deputy Deadbeat Daddy.

He was, at this point, the opposite of Bill Higgins.

Bill Higgins, who came out of retirement last year after the previous administration was finally exposed in its corruption, and who was reelected Mayor-President. It was a quirk of Baton Rouge politics that the Mayor of Baton Rouge was also the President of the Western Baton Rouge Parish, but it hardly mattered. Bill Higgins was king in this city. Hell, in this state.

And Carter wanted to align himself with such a man.

He needed to, if he had any hope of becoming mayor in eighteen months.

But he should have known better. He was an O'Neill, after all—scandal was practically his middle name. He thought that he could keep the dirty part of his life away from the clean part.

But honestly, when had he ever gotten what he wanted?

"You okay?" Amanda asked, and he realized he'd been silent far too long.

"How do we fix this?"

"Well—" Amanda leaned back in her chair "—we can get them to retract, but I'm not sure we can 'fix' what's really the issue here, Carter."

"Of course we can fix this. Anything can be fixed." He knew this for a fact. A lifetime of bribery and extortion, holding the worst of his family at bay like wolves in a storm, had taught him that everyone could be bought and anything worth fixing could be fixed.

Amanda stared at him as if he was something wiggling under a microscope.

"What?"

"Sometimes," she said, "you look like a different person. You get this expression and it's like I've never seen you before."

"Don't be ridiculous, Amanda."

"I'm not. I'm telling you, the mask you wear every damn day slips and the guy underneath it freaks me out a little bit."

He sighed. Amanda was great, but the frustrated novelist under her brittle public relations/press secretary exterior got a bit old. "What are we going to do about Zoe Madison?" he asked.

"The pregnant lady?" She waved a hand. "I can fix that. I can fix that in my sleep. What's got me worried is what's happening with your family.

The postponement of your father's arraignment is hurting us in public opinion. And you didn't tell me you testified for your mother ten years ago in a criminal case."

"Don't worry about it," he said, picking up the papers and dumping them in the recycling beside Amanda's desk.

"Worrying about it is kind of my job, Carter. I need an answer when those questions start coming up again, and they will if you're going to announce your candidacy for mayor after Christmas."

The sentence hung there, unanswered.

He was going to do that. That was the plan. The goal.

Yesterday, before his mother's resurfacing, it seemed like the fruition of years of hard work. The only likely outcome for his life.

Today, it seemed ridiculous. Announcing his candidacy for mayor while his father went to jail, his mother was snooping around in the shadows, and there was a missing ruby kicking around somewhere?

"That is still the plan, right?" Amanda asked.

"Yes," he said, because he still wanted it.

"Then don't put your head in the sand. We need a strategy and I need the truth."

"Our strategy," he said in a tone designed to remind her that she worked for him, "is that you say 'no comment.'"

"The public—"

"The attention will die down. It always does. We just need to stay the course."

"Stay the course?" She watched him dubiously. "This can't be you talking."

"What do you mean?"

"I mean, you haven't backed down from a fight once since taking this office. And now you want to stay the course? You think that's gonna work?"

"When it stops, *if* it stops working, we'll come up with a new strategy."

Amanda blew out a long breath, said, "You're the boss," and leaned back in her chair, kicking her feet up on the desk. "Now," she said, her eyes alight, "about Zoe Madison. We've got three choices. We can issue a statement saying you've never seen the girl and you are not the father."

"Will that work?"

"In time, but in that time, Blackwell's going to be going through your family's dirty laundry, of which there seems to be plenty. And sure, we can fight for some retractions, but it'll be like fighting a forest fire with a squirt gun."

"We need a distraction."

"Exactly. We can dig up a whole bunch of dirt and annihilate her in the press."

"Annihilate?" he asked, liking the idea.

"But she's practically picture-perfect. If we

go after her, it'll make us look like baby kitten killers."

"Okay, what's our second choice?" he asked, sorry to see annihilation off the table.

"Well, I've got an idea, and frankly it should take the heat off your shady family."

"Good," he said, ready for anything.

"Don't be too eager," she said. "This might hurt a little." There was something about Amanda's smile that made him nervous.

Very nervous.

THE PREGNANCY CRAVINGS were not to be messed with.

They were primitive and so strong they could last for days, taking Zoe places no sane woman should go.

She'd learned that the hard way in month three when she'd left the house in need of ice cream and had systematically torn the head off every person that had crossed her path. She'd made a four-year-old cry for accidentally riding her bike over Zoe's foot.

A four-year-old! Zoe was going to be a great mother.

Now, Zoe stayed home and rode the cravings out like she was tied to the saddle of a runaway horse. Or she called in reinforcements.

"You sure you're all right?" her mom asked,

wrapping one of Zoe's scarves around her neck. "That thing in the paper—"

"A huge misunderstanding, Mom," Zoe said, lying through her teeth. Her picture in the paper this morning had been a shocker, and that little trickle of guilt she'd been ignoring all night had turned into a geyser. She was on the front page of the paper and the story made it seem as though Carter O'Neill was one step down from an axe murderer.

Deputy Deadbeat Daddy. It was awful.

Well, some cold, no-nonsense voice in her head whispered, *what did you expect, standing on a chair like that?*

"The mayor's office will handle it, I'm sure," Zoe insisted, wanting her mother out of the house with such force it was hard not to just open the door and stand there, waiting for her to get the hint.

But Mom had brought salsa.

So she was trying to be polite.

"You sure you don't mind if I take this?" her mom asked, looking down at the green-blue ends of the scarf. "It looks so pretty on you."

It did. *It does.* It was her favorite scarf, but Mom needed to leave so Zoe could dunk her fresh batch of ginger cookies into the salsa in peace.

There were parts of this pregnancy business that required privacy, and this newfound obsession with ginger cookies and salsa was her own little secret.

"Absolutely, wear it in health. It goes great with your new hair," Zoe said, and as if cued, her mom smoothed a hand down the back of her new short silver bob.

"It does look good, doesn't it?" she asked, preening slightly in the mirror beside the door.

Go. Zoe thought. *Leave. Please.*

"You look much younger," she said instead.

Her mom beamed, tossing the scarf around her neck with a little flair, and Zoe smiled. "You don't look like you're about to be a grandmother, that's for sure," she said, feeling tubby next to her mom's hard-won thinness. Seven years ago, Mom had sworn she wasn't going to turn fifty in a size fourteen and she hadn't. She'd put her mind to it and lost twenty-five pounds. But that was Penny Madison for you. Once her mind was made up, that was it. Done. Deal. The weight had no choice but to leave in defeat.

"Okay," Penny said. "I need to get to work, but I'll see you tonight? We can go get a new slipcover for that couch."

"What's wrong with the scarf?" she asked, pulling on the pretty black fringe of the Spanish-style scarf that was draped over the back of her blue velvet couch. It had been part of a costume from

La Bohème adaption she'd done in Houston a few years ago.

"It looks a little trashy, sweetie. We'll get you something in a nice tweed."

Zoe didn't get a chance to say *over her dead body,* because her mom clasped her hands over Zoe's face, squeezing her cheeks just a little so that her lips pursed. An old routine her mom refused to let go of, despite the fact that Zoe was thirty-seven and five months pregnant.

You will always be my little girl, Penny was fond of saying. And somehow she always made it sound like a jail sentence.

"Okay," Zoe said, the words distorted by her squished face. "My last class is over at seven."

"I'll pick you up here at seven-thirty," her mom said, and pecked Zoe's pursed lips. "Remember," she said, her eyes flicking over to Zoe's kitchen counter, where a batch of ginger cookies sat getting cold. "Every pound you gain now is one you'll have to lose after the baby gets here."

Was it illegal to punch your mother? Zoe wondered, anger billowing through her. Or merely immoral? Because immoral she had no problem with. She was, after all, a political scandal in the making.

"Bye, honey," Penny said before Zoe could even curl a fist, and then she was gone. The Craving-

Goddess-turned-nightmare walked out the door, Zoe's favorite scarf trailing behind her.

"Oh, thank God," Zoe muttered and turned back to her cookies.

She cranked the lid off the jar of salsa and poured some into a chipped china bowl, because she wasn't a *heathen,* and then dunked the nearest cookie into the tomato mixture.

It was still disgusting, not a good fit at all. Salsa required salt, not sugar. Seriously, what possessed her? She eyed the cookie in her hand and dunked it again.

And why couldn't she stop?

A knock on the door practically shook the windows loose, and she quickly put down the cookie and slid the salsa into her fridge.

Wiping her hands and any stray crumbs from her face, she opened the door.

"Mom—"

But it wasn't her mom.

It was Carter O'Neill, in a suit and tie, dwarfing her doorway, his hands braced on the frame as if he were holding himself up. Or back.

Lord, he was big. Those muscles filling out his fine gray suit hard to ignore. And so were the blue eyes blazing through the distance between them.

It was Carter, all right. And he was pissed.

He stepped into her apartment without a word

and slammed the door shut behind him, turning her spacious apartment into a linen closet.

"We need to talk," he said.

CHAPTER THREE

"TALK?" SHE SQUEAKED, because the look on his face said that what he really needed was to take her out back and chop her into pieces.

He nodded, curt and decisive. His jawline was like the marble bust of a Roman emperor—all he was missing were the laurel leaves in his hair.

The truth was—her secret, hidden truth was—that there was something about a man in a suit. She had a history with men in suits. And this man wore a suit like no one else.

She pulled her faded silk robe tighter around her ballooning waist, as if to compensate.

He didn't say anything, didn't even acknowledge that he had in fact barged into her apartment uninvited. He just looked around as if he smelled something far worse than ginger cookies.

Anger trickled down through her spine, but the baby fluttered against her hand as if to say, *Hold on a second. He is Deputy Deadbeat Daddy because of you.*

"How did you get in here?" she asked. Someone had to buzz him in the main door.

"I helped Tootie Vogler with some groceries."

"I…ah…guess this is about the newspaper?" she asked.

His blue eyes burned like acid.

"Can I apologize again?" she asked. "I'm really, really sorry." He didn't respond, and her apology sat there between them like dog poop on a carpet.

"How…ah…did you find me?"

"Phone book."

"Right." Her laugh was awkward, and she wanted to take herself out back and end this misery. "Of course."

The silence was awful. It pounded between them, pulling her skin tighter, sucking out every molecule of air.

He was terribly out of place in the middle of her chaos, a dark spot, leaking menace like a fog into the center of the glitter and beads, the embroidered silk and pillows.

"Would you like to sit down?" she asked, pulling a bunch of pointe shoes and one of her more salvageable tutus off the pink-and-green watermelon chair. It was this chair or the velvet couch, with the much-maligned scarf.

His sharp blue eyes made her so nervous, so aware of the frivolity of her home, that she actually patted the seat in enticement.

Carter O'Neill, the cold fish, didn't even crack a smile.

"How about something to eat?" she asked. "I have ginger cookies. I just made them and there's some salsa in the fridge. Not that you'd want that together, obviously. But I have some chips. Somewhere."

He tossed the newspaper on the coffee table, carelessly knocking her favorite pig mug onto the rug. Luckily it was empty. She leaned over to pick it up and caught sight of herself, right there on the front page of the paper.

On a chair, a little blurry, but obviously pregnant. And frankly, the look on her face was pretty good, if she did say so herself. It managed to say it all—I loved you, but you hurt me so much that I can never forgive you.

All those acting classes her mother insisted on had really paid off.

Carter cleared his throat.

Right. Matter at hand. Political scandal.

"Are you involved with someone?" he asked.

"Involved?" she asked, yanked sideways by the question.

"Yes. Dating, or—" he heaved a big sigh, as if all this were a distasteful job "—whatever."

"No," she said.

"The father?" he asked, gesturing vaguely toward her stomach. "Is he around?"

"How in the world is that any of your business?" she asked, horrified.

"They're calling me Deputy Deadbeat Daddy," he said. "You kind of made it my business."

"I know," she whispered, guilt choking her. "I saw."

"Papers in Houston, New Orleans and *USA Today*," he said. "Did you see those, too?"

She blinked, her stomach in knots. She shook her head.

"All right, then how about you answer my question. The father—"

"Not…ah…" She got lost for a second in the absurdity of this conversation. "Around."

"That will make things easier."

Things like disposing of my body? she wondered. "Look, I didn't know there was a photographer there. Or that any of this would happen."

"Clearly," he said, his tone dubious.

"You don't believe me?"

"It doesn't matter what I believe. Or what you thought when you stood on that chair like a child and made up lies about me."

She gasped. She couldn't help it, it just came out.

"Don't you dare," he whispered, his voice and eyes, everything about him so suddenly menacing that she collapsed backward in the watermelon chair. He was gigantic; his hands could palm her head. He could make mincemeat out of her in a second. Not that she thought he would, but still…

"Don't pretend for a moment that you are in any way the injured party in this situation. You put us here." He pointed to the front page of the paper. "And you're going to do whatever I say to get us out."

Her eyes narrowed. Whatever he said? Not likely. "I can write a letter to the paper," she said. "Tell people that I'm off my meds, like you said. That I made it all up. Or we could just tell the truth, that someone paid me a thousand—"

"No," he said, his laugh not sounding like a laugh at all. "We won't be telling anyone the truth. Jim Blackwell is all over this like a dog on a bone."

"So…ah…what are we going to do?" she asked, suddenly light-headed with nerves.

"You," he said, pointing at her, pinning her to the chair, "are going to say nothing. To anyone. And we—" he waggled his finger between them "—are going to date."

For a moment, his words didn't make sense, and when they did she laughed. She laughed so hard she had to put a hand under her belly. And here she thought Carter didn't have a sense of humor.

"I'm not kidding," he said, stone-cold serious.

"You've got to be!" she cried. "There's no way

in the world anyone is going to believe that I am dating you!"

His face hardened, a cold mask that chilled her from across the room. Cruel and distant, his eyes raked her, pulled off her clothes, her skin.

Got it, she thought, pulling the tutu and mug against her chest as if the pig and the silk might keep her warm against the chill of him. *You wouldn't date me if I was the last woman alive. Message received.*

"Then why do this?" she asked, her voice a little shaky.

"Because," he said, "you've made me and this administration a laughingstock and the only way to bring back any legitimacy is to put our heads up and pretend like it was a bump in the road."

"What road?"

"Our road."

"We don't have a road! I stood up on a chair and…" She blinked, shook her head, something awful occurring to her. "People are going to think this baby is yours."

He stared at her as if she'd grown two heads. "They already do," he said. "And no one, no matter what we say, or whatever letter you write is going to believe otherwise."

"So how about we don't do anything. We lie low—"

"The news crew that's been following me around

all day followed me here. They're camped out on your front lawn."

"What?" she cried, whirling in her seat to peer through the light green sheers over her window. "Oh, my God," she whispered. He was right. A camera crew was loitering right in front of the main entrance to her loft building, smashing the bougainvillea Tootie Vogler had planted last year.

This is *not good*.

"Did they see you come in?" she asked, her voice so high it practically scraped the ceiling.

"They followed me, Zoe."

"You can leave out the back!" she cried. "Plead the fifth if anyone asks. Just pretend—"

"I'm a public official," he interrupted. "I can't lie low, and if this isn't addressed in some way, the speculation will only grow. And I can't let that happen," he said. "I won't."

For the first time in the brief twenty-four hours she'd known him, he seemed human. The ice in his blue eyes melted and revealed something vulnerable, as if he had something he cared about and might lose in this whole farce. His job.

"You like your job?" she asked.

He blinked, and after a long moment, he nodded. "I love my job. I have…work I want to do for this city."

Ah, man, why couldn't he go on being a jerk?

Now she was totally sunk—she couldn't be responsible for him losing his job.

"So we date?" she asked, still dubious.

He nodded. "We'll tell people I met you at one of the community center informational meetings. That I fell for your—"

Beauty? Charm? Too-big heart?

"Quirkiness. Your…ah…offbeat sense of humor. We'll tell them that stunt on the chair was your idea of a joke. Not a good one, but a joke. For a few months, we go on some very public dates. We get our photos taken and then you dump me."

Dumping him, she liked the sound of that. "What if I was married? Or in a relationship— like you said—"

"I knew you weren't married," he said. "But if you were involved in some other more informal relationship, our research might not have—"

"Research?" she interrupted, a cold chill spreading down her arms and across her chest. She stood, a toe shoe falling out of her hands, and she reeled it back in by the ribbon, reluctant to lose any of her armor. "You researched me?"

"Of course." He sounded as if he researched all of his dates. As if it made perfect sense.

"What exactly do you know?" she asked. "About me."

"You're thirty-seven, single." He arched one of those imperial blond eyebrows. "You were raised by Penny Madison, a single mother who works for the post office. You are—I guess were—a dancer. You recently moved back to Baton Rouge from Houston." She held her breath, a cold sweat blooming across her back. Was this happening? Did he know? Was her secret in a file somewhere, discussed at a meeting as though it was nothing? A bubble of nausea burned up her throat.

"You teach dance classes to kids and grand-parents," he said, leaving Houston and her secret behind. "And obviously…you're…ah…pregnant," he said, gesturing, embarrassed, at her belly, as if she were carrying a Shih Tzu in a dress instead of a baby.

"That's all?" she asked.

"Is there something more I need to know?" His blue eyes narrowed, sharp as knives.

"No." She edged around the blue couch to get as far away from him as possible. Unbelievably, she still felt the warmth from his body, like a distant sun. "That's my life," she muttered, wondering how something so full could be reduced to a few lines.

It occurred to her she didn't know anything about him. Not his age, not where he grew up. The lack of knowledge felt lopsided, but it's not as if it would ever occur to her to have him researched. Vetted.

She didn't work that way.

She looked at him, the compelling stillness of him, the cool of his eyes and the fine bones of his face. He was like nobility or something, a man removed from the messy realities of the kind of life she lived. Who looked, honestly, pained to be here with her. As if he were barely holding back all the disdain he felt for her.

This wasn't going to work. There was simply no way anyone would believe they *liked* each other, *desired* each other, *respected* each other—not for a minute.

"I know I made a mistake," she said. "I'm—" she swallowed and shook her head "—prone to that kind of thing, but look at you. You can barely stand to be here and, frankly, I don't like you being here. No one is going to believe that we're in a relationship."

Carter wiped his face and sat down on the edge of her coffee table. His knees a few inches from her legs, the edge of her silk robe trembled as if trying to get closer. "Look, we go out on a few dates. Get our picture taken. We make it…convincing."

"Convincing?" she squealed, wondering if that was code for sex. "I'm not sleeping with you."

He rolled his eyes. "We go to dinner, smile at each other. We hold hands."

"Hold hands?" She laughed. "Like we're teenagers? That's not going to convince anyone."

His hand, big and warm, stroked the kung fu

grip she had on her tutu. His thumb surfed the bumps of her knuckles and his fingers found her pulse, which jackhammered against her skin.

Touch. Warmth. He had calluses on the tips of his fingers, and the abrasion sent little shock waves through her body, waking up the parts of her that were hibernating during her long cold winter. Oh, lord, it had been so long.

Her blood slowed, turned to honey, as desire warmed in her belly.

The mug fell from her hand, thumping onto the carpet.

"I think we can make it work," he said, pulling his hand away and standing up, crossing to the far side of the room.

Golden sunlight burned through the windows, setting him aglitter. He was truly the most handsome man she'd ever seen, and that was saying something. It wasn't as though the Houston Ballet Company was filled with trolls.

Awareness and embarrassment buzzed through her, and she bent to pick up Sir Piggy as if the dollar store mug were her most prized possession.

The silence between them hummed, loud and awkward. He watched her, quiet. Waiting. But not smug—if he'd been smug, she would have chucked Sir Piggy right at his head.

But still, this reaction of hers, it wouldn't do. Not while he stood there, calm and collected, as unmoved by her as he'd been when he'd walked in the door.

"Okay," she said brightly, as if she weren't shaken down to her feet. "Public hand-holding it is. When do we start?"

"Tonight," he said, and her stomach plummeted. She'd been hoping for a few days, some time to get her head around this. To warn her mom and Phillip.

"What do I tell my friends?" she asked. "My mom."

"Nothing would be best."

"That's…that's not possible. They'll know this baby isn't yours. That we're not…together."

"That reporter—Jim Blackwell—he'll be all over your life, and that includes your family and friends. The less they know, the easier it will be on them."

Well, she thought, what was one more secret between her and her mother?

"All right. So where are we going tonight?"

"Bola," he said, naming the fancy steak house that had opened downtown a few months ago.

Nope. Uh-uh. Not going to happen. She would fake-date him anywhere but there. "I've heard it's awful," she lied.

He shook his head. "From who? The food there is amazing."

"Well, if it's amazing food you want, I know of a great soul food place down on River—"

"The point is to be seen by people," he said slowly, as if she were stupid. "Get our photo taken."

"But Bola has cockroaches," she whispered, as if Zagat were in the room with them. "In the kitchen."

"Are you trying to be funny?" he asked. "Because I really do not get your sense of humor. We're going to Bola."

Of course, she thought, resignation like a brick settling in her stomach. Maybe, if she was lucky, Phillip wouldn't be working.

At least the food would be good, she thought, happy to see a bright side. This baby loved steak. Zoe, of course, loved it dipped in cream cheese, but she would try to control herself.

"I'll pick you up at seven," he said.

"That won't work. I teach until seven and then… well, I'll need to get ready. Eight at the earliest." More like seven-fifteen at the earliest, but he didn't need to know that and he certainly didn't need to have every single thing go his way.

He nodded. "Eight then."

She managed to smile as if this were a real date, something to look forward to. "Eight it is."

Maybe it wouldn't be too bad, she thought, watching his long lean body cross the floor of her apartment. He was handsome, wealthy—at least she'd be able to eat a whole lot of steak in the next few months. Plus, he could hold hands better than most men made love. If she could just keep herself together and he managed to not be an autocratic ass, maybe everything would be all right.

Of course, there was Phillip to consider now, but she'd cross that bridge when she came to it.

"Try to wear something appropriate," he said.

And with that little ego crusher, he was gone.

CHAPTER FOUR

ZOE WAS RUNNING LATE. As usual. And Mom was not helping.

"No," she said, tucking the phone between her ear and her shoulder and locking the door behind her. She clicked on the lamp by the door and a puddle of warm light spread around her. "Mom, we're not...serious."

"But that thing in the paper, and now this? Dinner?"

"Yes, Mom, it's just dinner."

"At Bola? That's not *just dinner.*"

"It is. It's just a *fancy* dinner." A *fancy* dinner that required a *fancy* dress. "He's sort of a...*fancy* guy." She winced; that wasn't right at all. He was the opposite. He was stark and serious. *Fancy* like a rock face, maybe. Or an oak tree. She ran to her bedroom, shedding clothes as she went. Yoga pants—her pregnancy uniform—just weren't going to cut it tonight.

"And how long has this been going on?"

Zoe rolled her eyes and pulled open the accordion doors to her closet. "Not long," she said, yanking the ribbon attached to the small chain on her overhead light. She was trying to be vague, like Carter had told her, but her mom was like a hound dog. "A month, maybe. Honestly, we're just friends."

"Honey, why didn't you say something? I thought…" Penny trailed off, her voice leaving behind a little wake of pain mixed with guilt.

A delightful combination that her mother specialized in.

Zoe sighed and sat down on the mess of pillows and blankets she called a bed. She quickly bounced up and pulled a cereal bowl out from the duvet before settling back down. She didn't like lying to her mother, and she really didn't like hurting her, but at some point there needed to be some distance. Some breathing room.

Not for the first time, Zoe doubted her decision to come back to Baton Rouge to have this baby.

"I mean, you used to tell me everything. But recently, you're so different. The baby—"

She didn't want to talk about the baby with her mom. Not again. For four solid months it had been all they talked about, and now the subject was closed. Closed.

"Mom, listen to me. I sort of blew it with the whole standing on the chair thing, and now we have to go public. It's not a big deal."

"Why didn't you tell me?"

Zoe took a deep breath and jumped right into the new cold waters that swirled between them. "You know why, Mom."

"You're going to be a single mother, Zoe. Dating isn't—"

"And there you go," she said, standing up and wiggling out of her bra. "This is why I didn't tell you. I don't need another chapter from your *How To Be A Single Mother* textbook."

There was a pause, the silence long and slow, like colliding with an iceberg, and Zoe bit her lip to keep from apologizing. She was right on this.

"Do you like him?" Mom asked, her voice quiet. "Is he nice to you?"

Zoe nearly laughed. *Nice?* Carter O'Neill? The word simply did not apply. "Of course."

"All right, just…be careful with yourself, honey."

"I will. I have to go, Mom. Bye." Zoe hung up and tossed the phone on the bed.

She approached her closet like Napoleon taking over a battlefield. None of her pants fit, and she didn't have the money for new special maternity ones, so she shoved aside a small quadrant of black, white and denim pants. It wasn't a terribly formal sort of place so she pushed away the turquoise beaded gown and the black sheath from her days at the Houston Ballet. Ballerinas needed gowns for those fundraiser things, but why she still kept them she had no idea. Well, they were glittery and she *did* like glitter.

"This is a disaster," she moaned, flicking hangers back and forth, contemplating her pink cowboy shirt with the lassoing hearts. There was the red-and-white maternity tent dress her mother had bought her a few days ago, which honestly made her look like a tablecloth at an Italian restaurant. She pushed aside a few cardigans and dug way back into her closet, her heart sinking farther and farther into her stomach.

She wanted to look good tonight. Smokin', even. Because Carter had mocked her and had made her heart flip over in her chest when he'd held her hand.

The combination stung like salt in a wound.

But it didn't look like glamorous Zoe was going to make an appearance tonight. Or any other night for the foreseeable future. She was five months pregnant, a political prisoner of her own making, and she was attracted to the stone-cold warden.

Wedged into the back of her closet between her old prom dress and the remnants of her flapper phase, she found a clear plastic garment bag.

Sunshine dawned in her dark loft as she pulled out the hot pink raw silk A-line dress. A few years ago in Houston, she'd fallen in love with this dress, with its big red and yellow appliqué roses on the short hem, its bold color, and the way it made her legs look about a million miles long. The only problem was that it had been a little too big and she'd meant to have it altered, but kept forgetting.

Thank God.

She tore open the bag and pulled the dress over her head, shimmying it down around her belly and hips. She stepped sideways into the full-length mirror and squealed with delight. A little tight around the belly, but she was pregnant, what could one expect?

But the rest of it, oh the rest of it…perfect. The big collar clasped around her neck, a floppy silk rose beneath her chin. Her arms were bare, so she slid on a few silver bangles. And then a few more.

Shoes. Shoes would be an issue. Her swollen feet begged for the low sandals with the ghetto-fabulous gemstones, but she remembered how tall Carter was, how he seemed to tower over her, and she reached into the way back for her black second, secondhand Chanel stilettos.

Yes, she thought, admiring herself in the mirror. *Oh. Yes.* She pliéd, dipped. Tried to arabesque, but the seams wouldn't allow it. She felt beautiful in this dress.

Lush and womanly and sophisticated.

Like a woman who owned her life.

She could do this. She could go on this date and

hold hands and smile at a man who didn't like her at all. In this dress, she could do anything.

The walls of her apartment shuddered as someone pounded on her door. It could only be one person and she clapped.

"Eat your heart out, Carter O'Neill," she whispered and mini jetéd, as best she could, to the door.

"I'LL TRY TO BE THERE, Savannah," Carter said into his cell phone as he brushed the rain off his jacket.

"You're lying, Carter," his sister said. "I can tell. I can always tell. Honestly, why do you bother trying?"

Carter smiled, staring up at the ceiling. He liked it when his little sister called him on his bullshit; it made him feel closer to her, as though it was ten years ago and she still needed him to protect her.

He remembered her a year after their mom had left them on Margot's doorstep. Savannah had come into his room in the middle of the night, her voice a whisper, her hand against his arm a hot little puddle.

"She's not coming back, is she?" she'd asked, moonlight turning her eyes black. "Mom's left us here."

"I don't know," he'd whispered, though he'd

known. Of course he'd known. But he hadn't wanted to hurt her. He hadn't wanted any more injury to befall this little girl.

"You're lying," she'd said. "You're always lying to me."

Suddenly, in this hallway, Carter felt a million miles from his sister. From his family. From the man he was. And it was his own fault. Every time he tried to protect them he ended up putting more than miles between them.

"Savvy," he sighed, "I promise I will try to get there for Christmas."

Even as the words came out of his mouth he knew it was impossible. With Vanessa back in the picture, there was no way he could go home, not with her trailing behind like a spiked tail.

"Hey," he said, unable to believe he was going to ask this question when he'd sworn to himself that he was going to stay out of the gem drama. "You guys haven't found the ruby, have you?"

"Tyler hunted all over the place last month when Dad was here. He says it's nowhere to be found."

"What does Margot say?" he asked.

"She says there's no way it's in The Manor. She'd know."

"Well, she sure as hell didn't know about the diamond, did she?"

"I guess not," Savannah said. "She was as surprised as the rest of us when Tyler said he found it and Dad stole it from him."

"Is Margot there?" he asked.

"She's in West Palm Beach with her boyfriend."

"Oh, come on," he said, trying to scrub the mental picture of his grandmother with a boyfriend.

"Don't be such a prude. They're companions."

"Has anything strange happened at The Manor lately?"

"Not more than usual."

There, he thought, he'd satisfied the worry his mother had planted in his brain. He could go on with his life.

"How is Katie?" he asked. It was easier in a way to stay apart from The Manor, Bonne Terre and his family. When he didn't see them for months at a time, he couldn't picture them at the breakfast table, going to school, getting ready for bed, couldn't think of his niece, Katie, growing up and him not seeing it.

He didn't have to think about all the things he was missing.

"If you really cared, Carter, you'd come see her."

It was a direct hit, and his body stung with shame that quickly fizzed and exploded to anger. His life wasn't that simple. Had never been that simple. From the moment Savannah came into this world he'd been protecting her, watching over her, doing everything in his goddamned power to make sure that her life *was* that simple.

Carter turned and hammered on Zoe's door, using the side of his fist.

"I'll call you soon," he said, and hammered again. What was taking Zoe so long? he wondered. She lived in like a one-room loft.

"Think about Christmas," Savannah said, subdued, as if she knew she'd pushed too hard.

"I will," he said, and heard the door behind him rattle, the chain lock being lifted. "Gotta run."

He felt the door give and he turned, dropping his phone in his pocket. "Good God, Zoe, it took you—"

The world narrowed down to one color. One hot pink blast of color that seared his eyes, harpooned his brain. There was no other color like it. Ever. In his life.

"—long enough," he finished lamely. The color belonged to a dress, a short one and he couldn't believe it, but Zoe the pregnant elf had legs that hit the ceiling and met the floor in a pair of heels that made his heart pound in his crotch.

"Hi," she said, and he jerked his eyes up to hers. They were smiling, the green depths aglow with a feminine confidence that zinged through his blood stream. She knew she looked good.

The desire was a huge surprise. An unwelcome one, like being cut off at the knees.

"Hello" he answered, trying to cool himself down, pull himself away from the magnetic allure of her.

Of that damn dress.

"Ah…" She blinked, her confidence crumpling slightly. "Give me one more second." She swirled a finger around her face.

He nodded and she trotted off to a dark corner of her loft, leaving him in the dimly lit doorway. He stepped inside and closed the door behind him. She had lamps everywhere, some covered by scarves, casting a rosy glow over the wood floors and high white walls.

She was a candle person, he just knew it.

"So," she yelled, "did you come in the back?"

"Nope," he answered, picking up a framed photograph of a young girl in a sequined dance costume, her smile revealing two missing front teeth.

Zoe, he could tell by the eyes. The exuberance with which the girl smiled, like her whole body was required to do it right.

"Were the photographers still there?" she asked, ducking her head out a doorway. She was using some kind of contraption on her eyelids, a cage or something.

"Yes," he said.

"They were gone when I came home tonight," she said.

"Because they were following me," he said, having spent the day feeling like Britney Spears.

She grimaced. "That's no fun."

He nearly laughed at her understatement. Nothing about this was fun, except maybe looking at her legs.

"All right," she said, stepping into the hallway. She grabbed a tiny pea-green bag off a small table and emerged from the shadows. "I'm ready for steak."

She was lovely, more than lovely, really. She was like a rare creature. All eyes and legs and lips. Her black hair shone like an oil slick, and her skin glowed as if there were a candle burning inside her.

If this were a real date, he'd say something now. Kiss her hand and breathe a compliment across her skin. Truthfully, if this were a real date he'd back her into those shadows and up against a wall and he'd explore the secrets of those endless legs. Thinking about it, his fingers twitched. His pulse hitched.

But this wasn't a date, and this woman was doing a number on his reputation and future political career.

"Good," he said, brusquely, holding open the door for her. "Bring a coat. It's raining."

They went down the stairs and in the main hall-way she turned left to head for the back door but he stopped her. "We're going out the front."

She leaned out of the corridor, looking at the small crowd of photographers visible through the safety glass door.

"Really?" she asked, clearly hesitant.

"It's sort of the point."

"But—" she licked her lips, her fingers fluttering over her belly "—can't we go slow or something?" she asked. "Ease into it?"

He shook his head, but faced by her nerves and beauty he found himself weakening. He took her hand where it rested against the swell of her stomach. He tried not to, but he couldn't help briefly noticing the taut warmth of that belly.

A baby, he thought. There's a baby in there.

"You're going to be fine," he said. "Just smile."

She didn't smile. Didn't joke. He realized she was really rattled. "You okay?" he asked, stroking the chilled skin of her wrist.

"Tell me something," she said. "Anything. About yourself."

"What?"

"You know everything about me. Well, not everything, but lots. Lots more than I know about you."

"Why does that matter?" he asked.

"Because we're supposed to be dating!" she cried. "And you're holding my hand, and they're going to take pictures of us, and we're supposed to make it convincing. And I think maybe that convincing needs to start right now. With me. So spill, Carter. Give me something."

"I…ah…have a younger sister," he said, not entirely sure why he was indulging her. "And a brother."

"You do?" she asked, her eyes wide.

"Why is that such a surprise?"

"I don't know." She smiled and shrugged one elegant shoulder. "You seem kind of like a lone wolf, you know. Not exactly the big brother type."

Oh, but he was. He was a big brother, all the way down to his core.

And if that meant staying away from his family in order to keep his mother away from them, no matter how much it might hurt him—then so be it. He could handle it. Because he knew better than to take something he wanted. He lived every minute of his life under sublimation of want. Compromise of need.

Christmas was simply another day. Another day without his family.

"Carter?" she asked. Her hand, no longer chilled, squeezed his.

"I miss them," he said and felt as if he'd jumped off a cliff, nothing but air under his feet. He cleared his throat, wishing he could suck the words back into his mouth.

But Zoe's smile was wide and sincere and some of the confidence bloomed back into her eyes, making the green shine bright. Lovely, he thought, slightly spellbound. So lovely.

"All right," she said, and took a deep breath. "That's good stuff to know. We can go now."

She grabbed his hand and tugged, pulling him down the narrow hallway to the front door where the flashbulbs and journalists waited like sharks in shallow water.

They pushed through the front door and the flashes exploded. Zoe stumbled slightly and lifted a hand to cover her eyes.

"Oh wow," she whispered, sounding lost.

It wasn't totally an act when he put his arm around her, curling her toward him.

"Mayor Pro Tem?" someone shouted. "Are you the father of the baby?"

Zoe stiffened, a fire igniting in her eyes. It was ugly, the speculation about the baby, and he wished, oddly, that he could spare her some of that—despite the fact that she'd brought it on herself, however unwittingly. She opened her mouth, no doubt about to get them deeper into trouble, and he squeezed her arm.

"The father of Zoe's baby is no one's business but Zoe's," he said.

"How long have you two been dating?" another person shouted and Carter glanced down at Zoe.

"Five minutes?" she whispered, and he laughed. Flashbulbs exploded again.

"A few weeks," he finally said. "Now, if you'll excuse me, we're going to get some dinner."

Questions were hurled after them, but he ignored them. Why he kept his arm around Zoe, he wasn't entirely sure.

SHE'D NEVER BEEN TO BOLA, but what Phillip had told her didn't do the place justice.

Bola was gorgeous, if one liked art deco, red velvet and mahogany floors, and Zoe did. The dark lighting made her want to purr and sashay across the floor, a mink trailing behind her. She could imagine Carter, his blond hair slicked back, his big shoulders tucked into one of those exquisite tuxes from the era.

Oh, yes, she could imagine that very well. Perhaps a boutonniere, a white rose, pinned right onto that impressive chest of his. She'd pat that chest, trail one blood-red nail along his lapel—

Her stomach growled like a semi roaring to life, ruining the image.

Embarrassed, she glanced over at Carter to see if he noticed. He stared at her, blank faced.

"Was that *you?*" he asked as they followed the white-jacketed waiter to their table.

"I'm hungry," she protested.

"Clearly," he muttered, but his eyes twinkled, and Carter with twinkling eyes was a very fine sight.

"Your table," the waiter said, and as Zoe slid past him, she whispered, "Is Phillip working tonight?"

The waiter nodded and Zoe's baby did a worried backflip. "He is. Would you like me to send him over?"

"Dear God, no," she whispered vehemently and then smiled at the man's slightly stunned expression. "Thanks, though."

He bowed and left.

"So, should we just have them bring the cow?" Carter asked, glancing at the menu.

And a vat of cream cheese, she thought.

"Just part of it," she managed to say with a smile. "You…ah…handled those reporters really well," she said, searching for conversation now that they were here at the table with a dinner to get through. He'd been on the phone the whole car ride over, talking to someone named Amanda about retractions.

"You get used to it in politics."

"Maybe you should give me some tips," she said. "You know, so I don't blow it."

"Tell them some truth, but not all of it. Keep them wondering. That sort of thing. But you did great, tonight. Very charming," he said, his smile brief but beautiful, revealing all that potent glamour he hid away.

Phillip was going to lose his marbles.

"I didn't say anything."

"That's what was so great."

Sticking out her tongue seemed like the right reaction, but she wasn't entirely sure that wasn't the hormones.

Carter's pocket buzzed and he dug out a cell phone the size of a deck of cards. He glanced at the screen and winced. "I need to take this," he said and left the booth without glancing back at her.

She blinked, taken aback by his rudeness.

If this relationship were real, the cell phone would be the first thing to go, she thought.

"Can I get you something to drink while you wait to order?" the waiter asked when he approached their table, like a polite ghost ready to disappear at the shake of her head.

"I'm ready to order," she said. "We'll both have the porterhouse. Bloody. And potatoes."

"Baked? Scalloped?"

"Both," she said. "And we probably need something green." She patted the baby, who was clamoring for cream cheese.

"Our vegetable today is asparagus."

"Perfect."

The waiter blinked and nodded. "Drinks?"

"Water is fine," she said, taking a sip to prove it. "But bring him something fruity. With an umbrella."

The sillier the better.

The waiter smiled and vanished, only to reappear with a bread basket—bless him—and winked before vanishing once more.

She caught a few interested looks and some very dark glances being thrown her way from other diners, but she just tried to appear Zen as she covered a roll with butter.

Bola was busy and getting busier. Perhaps Phillip wouldn't have a chance to take a break and come find her. He didn't know she was here, after all. Would never in this life expect it.

"This is a joke, right?"

No such luck.

"Hi, Phillip," she sighed.

CHAPTER FIVE

PHILLIP, GORGEOUS in his white jacket and some tasteful guyliner, stood beside her table, using tongs to replenish her still-full bread basket.

"I've been trying to call you all day long," he said.

"I've been avoiding you."

"Obviously. Are you actually dating Deputy Deadbeat Daddy?" he asked, his voice climbing above the muted din that filled the restaurant. "And you didn't tell me?"

Zoe glanced behind him for a sign of Carter, but he was nowhere to be found.

"I know, I should have answered—"

"Damn right you should have answered." He radiated anger and her bread basket was about to overflow but Phillip wasn't about to walk away. He managed to place one more rye knot on top of her leaning tower of carbohydrates.

"Is this...relationship between you and Carter O'Neill for real?" he asked, dropping his outrage. Now he was just Phillip, her best friend since dance class in the fifth grade.

"Carter and I are just…friends," she said, the lie falling awkwardly from her mouth like a big fat rock.

He stared at her askance, and she tried to keep her face as composed as possible, like in those books when people are trying to stop psychics from reading their minds by thinking of beaches or something. That was her, trying not to let on that the whole situation was out of her control and freaking her out.

"Uh-uh," he said. "I'm not buying that for a minute, sugar. Is he—" Phillip glanced behind him, but still no Carter, and leaned down "—the father?"

"No!" She practically shrieked. "Good God, no."

Phillip stared at her for a long time, his black eyes acute and concerned. "I know you're convinced you're not *lying* when you won't tell anyone who the father is, but it feels like I'm being lied to."

Sadness pinged through her, ricocheting off shame and embarrassment. This baby wasn't even born and was already so scandalous.

"Carter is not the father," she said, refusing to let the guilt budge her from her decision to keep her baby's father a secret. She had a plan, damn it, and she was sticking to it.

"Then tell me, honey, what is going on?"

She couldn't tell him. Shouldn't.

Phillip traded his bucket of fancy bread for a silver pitcher of water from another passing waiter. "This isn't another one of your follow-your-heart moments, is it? Because last time you dated one of these suit guys he wanted to change you—"

Mute, Zoe watched Phillip fill her glass with water.

The problem with best friends, she thought, *is that they know too much.*

"Carter doesn't want to change me," she whispered. *He doesn't even know me. Or like me.*

It was killing her not to tell him, and she realized that Phillip wasn't going to go run off to *USA Today* and spill their secret. Phillip wasn't like that. He was her friend, and frankly, she needed a friend right now. "Listen, I shouldn't tell you this, but—"

"Zoe."

Carter was back, standing right behind Phillip, making her friend's own spectacular glamour seem somehow childish. That was the thing about Carter—all other men seemed like boys around him.

"Enjoy your bread," Phillip said, glaring at Carter as he walked away.

Carter sat, folding his napkin into his lap with precision. "Who was that?" he asked.

"Phillip," she said, feeling as though she'd been caught doing something wrong. "My friend."

"You were going to tell him?" he asked.

"It's not like he's a reporter," she said. "He doesn't even know any reporters."

"Trust me, by tomorrow, he'll know a bunch of them." He reached out his hand, touching her fingertips with his own and then retreating, leaving her skin tingling.

She was annoyed by and attracted to the man—a gross combination.

"Is this the hand-holding part of the evening?" she asked, feeling miserable.

His smile was so surprising, it disarmed her right out of her misery. "No," he said, shaking his head. "Why don't we order?"

"I already did," she said and his eyebrows shot up.

"What am I having?" he asked, and she couldn't tell if he was angry. The phone at his elbow buzzed and he glanced at the screen, his body poised to stand up.

"You know, if you really want to convince people that we're dating, you'd turn that thing off for an hour or two."

"I don't ever turn my phone off," he said, staring at her as if she'd asked him to take off his clothes and dance the hula.

"Ever?"

"I turn the ringer off, but no, I never turn off my phone. I'm the mayor pro tempore of a major metropolitan city."

Zoe sat back, seeing Carter in a new way. A sad new way. "That's not all you are," she asked, "is it?"

He blinked, his eyes heavy and dark for just a moment, as if he understood the truth of what she'd said, and then he grabbed his phone. "This is my world, Zoe, and you're only passing through. Don't make judgments on things you don't understand. I'll be right back."

Zoe's entire body flushed and buzzed with anger and embarrassment. She just got a dressing-down from her fake date.

"Well," she muttered, grabbing another roll. "No wonder he's alone."

A few moments later he was back. He hesitated at her chair, his fingers brushing her shoulder and sending sparks down her body, straight to her breasts.

Down, girls, she thought, sternly. *Those fingers are all wrong for you.*

"I'm sorry," he said. "I shouldn't have snapped at you."

"Probably not," she said. "If this were a real date, I would have left."

His chuckle was dry. "It wouldn't be the first time a date left me."

She gaped at him. "And you're okay with that?"

"I love my job, Zoe, and I've never met a woman that made me want to put my work second."

"Hmm," Zoe murmured, wondering why that sounded noble. Sexy, even. As though he was just a hardworking man looking for the right kind of woman.

Her hormones, absolutely out of control with baby power, really liked Carter in that light—as if he was the hero in a romance novel and she was the young virgin secretary there to change his life.

Zoe crossed her legs and tried to think of smelly pointe shoes. Dancing on broken toes. Blisters. "What are all the phone calls about? Mayoral espionage? Is New Orleans trying to take our land?"

He laughed. "I wish. Actually, I don't wish. I'm getting some personal funding for the Glenview Community Center debacle, and I think the deal is getting pretty close to going through."

"Oh," she said, her roll forgotten in her hands. He needed to stop doing that. Just when she'd convinced herself she didn't like him, no matter how good he looked in a suit, he confessed to fixing a community center debacle. "That's good."

"It's great," he said, leaning back, his jacket sliding open to reveal his trim waist in a crisp white shirt.

Delicious, she thought, which was ridiculous but

true nonetheless. She kind of wanted to dip him in cream cheese.

"With that community center being finished, hopefully we can get some more community support to repair the centers that need it. Get some much-needed programs up and running in underserviced neighborhoods."

"The lights didn't work in my room at Jimmie Simpson today," she said. "I had my toddlers dancing outside in the ball diamond."

"That's what I mean," he said. "If we want to cut down on crime and vandalism and increase our graduation rates, we need to give kids a place to go besides the street. It's the only way to curb the total downward spiral our teenage population is currently experiencing. Without programs that interest kids and plug them into something positive—and without a place to have those programs—I don't know how to turn things around."

She stared at him, spellbound. Mesmerized by his passion.

Did she think Carter O'Neill was cold? Fool. He was fire under ice. He was crimson coals, waiting for the chance to ignite.

"Sorry," he said, after a moment. The passion banked, vanished. Like it never was. It was quite a trick, as disarming as his smile. "I get carried away."

"You're right to," she said. "We should all get carried away about this."

"Why don't you tell me about dance?" he asked.

She laughed. "What about it? The history? The modern movement? Teaching two-year-olds?"

"You," he said, leaning forward, slicing away the rest of the world with the sharpness of his focus. "Tell me about dance and you. About Houston."

"I was a part of the ballet company there," she said. "For three years."

"Did you like it?"

"Like it?" She smiled and then laughed. "I loved it. It was everything I had worked for since I was four. The artistic director was a genius, and fair-minded. The company had its drama but for the most part we believed in what we were doing. And the city loved us. It was a dream."

"And now you teach two-year-olds." She stiffened at his tone but chose to laugh it off. It might seem like she'd fallen down in the world, but this was a choice. Everything that led her to this moment and place in her life had been a choice.

And teaching dance was a choice she'd made at a young age. A greater calling than being on the stage. A passion far brighter than her star had been.

"Let's not forget my seniors samba class."

"How could I?" His smile took away the sting.

"And is that what you want?" he asked, all joking aside. "To teach."

"It's all I want," she said, surprised that she was telling him this. She hadn't expressed this to her mother, or even Phillip, afraid that they would laugh at her or think she was lying to save face. But Carter just leaned in, his eyes alive with interest, and she found herself unleashing her plans, her dreams. "I love it. Even more than I love dancing myself and when...well, hopefully, in a few years I can get the money together, and I plan to start an academy."

"The Zoe Madison School of Dance?"

"Something like that. A permanent building. I've got my eye on one off St. Louis Street, a nice storefront with lots of space and it's central, right by bus stops and the highway. I can do all types of classes for all ages. Scholarship programs and maybe even ties to local gymnastic groups. I want it to be a dance community, for anyone interested in being a part of it. I can—" She stopped, her tongue suddenly too big for her mouth. She felt her cheeks incinerate with high heat. "Sorry," she mumbled, echoing his words. "I get carried away."

His smile was like booze—too much of it and she'd be drunk.

"Your passion is exciting," he said and cleared

his throat, glancing down at the tablecloth. "Infectious."

He opened his mouth as if to ask something else, but shut it, second-guessing himself.

"What?" She laughed.

"I don't want to pry—"

She tipped back her head and howled. "We're fake-dating, Carter. Ask what you want, I won't guarantee an answer, but let's not make this more complicated than it needs to be."

"Fine. Why did you leave?" he asked. "Houston, I mean. You're young. You obviously loved it. Why come back here?"

She blinked at him. "I'm pregnant."

"Yeah, but I'm sure other ballerinas have had babies and kept dancing. And Houston has a bigger market for an academy like the one you dream about."

"Maybe," she said. "But I was alone in that city. My mother, my real friends, the ones I could count on to help, were all here."

"The father…?" He trailed off then held up his hand. "I know. None of my business."

She smiled, toying with her water glass.

"What's so funny?"

"You're the only person in my life who seems to respect that concept."

"Well, reporters can be relentless."

"Reporters have nothing on my mom."

Now he blinked. "You haven't told your mother?"

Her anger spiked and she pushed away her glass. "I don't understand why this is so hard for people to get. The first person I'm going to tell is my baby. It's our lives. I mean, am I crazy? Isn't that what makes sense?"

He didn't answer for a long time.

"It is crazy," she muttered.

"I think it's laudable," he said and cleared his throat, fiddled with his tie. Carter was cute when he was uncomfortable. "Respectful. Of your child, of that relationship. It says a lot about you."

"That I'm crazy."

"Oh, you're crazy," he said with a laugh, and somehow it didn't seem like such a bad thing when he said it that way. "But not for this."

Her body buzzed. Her hormones did a long slow rumba through her veins.

"No one has said that," she murmured.

And she wished, so badly, that they would. And now, here was this man she didn't want to like— reaching into her head.

This dating business wasn't going the way she thought it would. She thought a fake date would be business-like, that they'd talk about the weather or professional sports. Good God, she didn't want to bond with the man.

"Tell me something," she said.

"Oh, boy."

"That blond woman?" she said, "who paid me all that money?" She pushed past the tension in his face, the chill in his eyes. "Who is she?"

"She's no one," he said. "Absolutely no one."

"Porterhouses?" Their waiter arrived from no-where and started to unload a giant tray of food.

"Holy…is this all ours?" Carter asked as the baked and scalloped potatoes hit the table.

"Welcome to my world," she said.

And dug in.

CARTER WALKED ZOE UP to her door, his hand cupping her elbow like he was holding a little fire in his palm.

"You know if teaching dance stops working for you, I think you could go cross-country and enter eating contests. You like pie, right? Hot dogs?"

She tried to look offended but he just laughed.

"I have never in my life seen someone eat like you just did."

"I am going to choose to take that as a compli-ment," she said, sticking her little nose in the air. It was cute. She was cute.

She was funny and opinionated and elegant and goofy.

A combination he hadn't seen in a woman in

years. This fake date, this task he'd had to take on, had begun to feel good. And his irritation with the elf had turned into something else entirely.

Maybe it was watching her put away all that steak.

He liked her. Was intrigued by her.

"Where are all the reporters?" she asked as they climbed the steps to her apartment building unbothered. "Maybe we're already old news."

"Don't be too sure," Carter said. "They might be lurking in the bushes."

"I doubt it," she said, pausing in front of the glass security door. "I think in terms of scandals we're pretty tame these days."

"Maybe you're right," he said, turning to face her.

The moonlight slashed through the courtyard, cutting ribbons of white out of the darkness and her eyes glimmered in the half-light.

She licked her lips, leaving them damp, and the moment melted into steam and heat.

"I didn't tell you how beautiful you look," he whispered.

"No," she said. "You didn't."

"I should have."

Her mouth opened. Closed. The sounds of crickets deafening in the sudden silence. Her hands smoothed over her belly. God, his need to touch her. To grab her even—it was nuts. He'd never in his life felt this way. Compelled.

Like he wanted to open his mouth and inhale her.

And before he knew it, before he could stop it, he was leaning down to kiss her. His fingers slid from her elbow to the fine skin of her neck.

Velvet. Every inch of her was velvet.

"Carter," she whispered, her lips inches from his.

"Yes."

"I don't usually do this."

"Me neither."

"It's the hormones," she said. "The pregnancy. They're making me crazy."

He laughed and, oddly, it didn't ruin the mood. "Okay."

"And your suit. I love a man in a suit."

"I have lots."

"And the steak—"

"Zoe?"

"Yes?"

"Can I please kiss you?"

Her smile illuminated the darkness, a neon sign in the midnight sky. "Yes," she sighed.

He'd never kissed a woman while smiling and it was a hot sweetness. Honey on his lips, fire on his tongue.

And then the night exploded in flashbulbs. The

whirr and click of cameras. Zoe jerked away, stumbling slightly and he grabbed her to hold her steady, his palms melting into her skin.

"Give us a kiss, Zoe!" yelled the scum-sucking paparazzo standing in the shadows beside the bushes.

Zoe flinched, and even in the moonlight he could tell all the color had leeched from her skin.

Her eyes, vulnerable and angry, crushed him.

"I didn't know that guy was there," he said, but she pulled her elbows into herself, becoming tiny against the night as she slipped away from him.

"Come on, sweetie, don't be mad!" the photographer yelled, and Zoe ducked her head, fumbled in her pea-green bag for her keys. Her fingers shook and tears poised themselves on the edge of her eyelashes.

"Zoe—"

The door cracked open and she was gone. A flash of pink, a long leg and he was alone in the night, his blood hammering hard through his body.

"Not your night, huh?" Jim Blackwell emerged from behind the bushes like the devil stepping into the light.

Don't hit him. You can't hit him.

Hitting him would only make things worse.

But the urge was a wild dog at his heels.

"No comment?" Jim asked.

"Go to hell, Jim," Carter said and walked away, his night in ruins around him.

CHAPTER SIX

"DEPUTY DEADBEAT DADDY Denied?" Amanda asked as she walked into the office on Monday morning. She tossed the paper onto Carter's desk so he could see, once again, the photo on the front page.

There he was, in bright crisp and clear color, leaning in, eyes closed, lips pursed—puckered up, really, like a child. But that wasn't even the best part of the photo—no, the look on Zoe's face as she leaned away from him, as if Carter were made of stinky cheese—*that* was the best part of the photo.

"It gets worse," Amanda said.

"USA Today?"

"No, YouTube. The photographer got video. Deputy Deadbeat Daddy Denied is worldwide right now."

"Great," he muttered, spinning in his chair to face the window. Outside it was a gorgeous day, blue skies, fluffy white clouds—everything mocked him.

Why did I try to kiss her? he wondered, feeling thick and heavy. This wasn't supposed to be real.

She wasn't supposed to be so damn real.

One of the most real things he'd experienced in a long time.

He had no idea what she was thinking about right now, and he hated that he wondered. That he cared.

Stupid was the word. He felt stupid.

"I'll deal with it," he said.

"How?"

I'm not sure yet, he admitted to himself.

"I have a meeting with Eric Lafayette in an hour about the Glenview—"

"You can't just brush this off," Amanda snapped. "Eleven months until elections, Carter. You want a life in public service, you need to handle this crap. Pretending it's not happening isn't going to make it go away."

"I'm not. I said I'd deal with it, and I will."

"Carter, I'm on your side. I can help."

"You want to call Zoe and explain that the kiss wasn't a promotional stunt?" he snapped.

"Er...no?"

"Then we're done here."

After a long moment Amanda got the point and left.

Zoe's stink face stared up from the paper and he couldn't take it anymore.

He pulled out his cell phone and faced the music.

ZOE'S CELL PHONE RATTLED against her kitchen counter, and her heart did a similar dance against her rib cage.

She didn't know why she was so nervous, or frankly, how she knew it was Carter calling.

But she was nervous and it was him.

"You want me to talk to him?" Penny asked, ready to rush to Zoe's defense, as though they were on the playground and Carter pushed her off the slide.

"I can handle this, Mom," she said, though she was slightly afraid she couldn't. She'd woken up this morning to Penny and the front page of the paper.

A combination that had her running for the ginger cookies and salsa and she didn't care who saw.

It was bad, being kissed for a publicity stunt, but it was far worse to have that kiss all over the front page of the paper. And she wasn't even the one that looked bad.

Poor Carter.

His pride must be sore this morning.

She scooped up the phone and answered it as she walked into her bedroom and some privacy.

"Hello," she said, cool as a cucumber.

"Zoe, it's Carter."

"Good morning," she said, channeling every

aloof and distant receptionist she'd ever come across.

"Zoe." He sighed, and she heard the frustration in his voice, a certain weariness that pulled at her.

Do not fall for that again, she told herself. *This is a man you are fake dating. That's it.*

"You've seen the paper?" he asked.

She nodded then realized how stupid that was. "Yes," she said. "I have."

"I didn't know that photographer was there," he said.

"Really?" she asked, not at all cucumber-like. "He just happened to burst out from behind the bushes the moment we…kiss?" she whispered the last word, sure her mother was eavesdropping. Not that Penny didn't know about the kiss; Zoe just didn't want to talk about it with her mom listening.

"I had no idea," Carter said. "I promise."

Promise? she thought. Something about Carter making a promise to her seemed authentic. It wasn't something he would do lightly.

If it wasn't a stunt, that meant the kiss was real. Genuine.

And somehow that was worse. She didn't know what to do with those feelings. There was no slot in her life for wanting to kiss Carter.

"And if I really wanted to catch you in some kind of compromising position, it backfired—"

"Terribly," she agreed. Then, because the photo was so awful, and the situation so ridiculous, she started to laugh.

"Are you laughing at me?" he asked.

"Yep," she said, and laughed some more. Some of that strange magic from last night lingered on her skin, the tips of her hair. She felt young and giddy.

"It is a bad photo," he admitted, and she could almost hear the smile in his voice.

"The worst!"

She turned and sat on the edge of her bed and saw her mother standing in the doorway, her face cut into stern, unforgiving lines.

Zoe's laughter died in her throat.

The magic vanished, and she felt like a teenager caught doing something wrong.

She plucked at the knee of her yoga pants.

"So?" she asked, terribly aware of her mother's eyes, her judgment. Even more aware that her mother, standing there with all the experience of a single parent, was probably right.

Zoe had no business worrying about Carter O'Neill's promises. Or teasing him. She was going to have a baby in a few months; she needed to focus on that.

"Are we done?" Zoe asked. "No more dates?"

"Not yet," he said. "I have to do a little more damage control after Deadbeat Daddy Denied."

She ignored the little zing of excitement, smothered it with all kinds of worry and anxiety. More fake dates. More photos. More hand-holding.

"What…ah…what's next?" She had no idea where mayor pro temps went on a second fake date.

"The National Ballet is in town."

Oh, he was hitting her where it hurt. She would give her teeth to go see the ballet.

"How about Wednesday evening," he said. "We'll get some dinner—"

"No dinner," she said. She had made Carter a promise, but her mother was right; dating right now, fake or not, was a distraction she didn't need. If this was business, she would keep it business.

"I'll meet you there," she said. Her mother made a disgusted noise and vanished from the doorway, leaving her alone in the sunny silence of her room.

She cleared her throat, lowered her voice. "And no…no more kissing."

Carter was silent a long time and Zoe's heart pounded in her ears. "I wanted to kiss you, Zoe," he said, his voice gruff. "I didn't fake it and I certainly never expected it."

"I know," she said. Being noble sucked. "I didn't, either, but…this relationship isn't real and never could be, or would be if I hadn't created such a bizarre situation."

"I agree."

"Great," she said, bright as day. "Then let's keep it businesslike."

Carter's laugh made her smile and her heart twist. "Something tells me, Zoe, that you wouldn't know businesslike if it came up and bit you on the nose."

"You're right," she agreed. "But you do, so I'll follow your lead."

"What if businesslike isn't all I want?" he asked and she nearly melted in response.

"Then you are fake-dating the wrong woman," she said. "Because that's all I've got right now."

Please, she added silently, *don't push. Don't make this harder than it is.*

"Okay. I'll see you Wednesday. I'll call you with details."

Zoe disconnected and stared at her phone in her palm, wondering what she'd gotten herself into. One thing was for sure, she had to tell her mother the truth about this fake-dating situation— there was no other way to avoid the lecture of a lifetime.

She pulled together her courage and went out into the kitchen where her mother was using a wicked sharp blade to pulverize a bunch of apples.

"What are you doing?" Zoe asked carefully.

"Making applesauce," she answered, then slammed down the blade, and Zoe jumped. "The question is, what are you doing?"

"It's nothing, Mom." When Penny opened her mouth to respond Zoe held up her hand and told her everything. About the newspaper. The arrangement. Carter's career. All of it.

"See, Mom," she said, looking forward to getting her mother off her back. "It's one hundred percent nothing."

"Look at you," Mom said. "You're lying to yourself."

"What are you talking about?" Zoe sighed. Apparently she hadn't avoided the lecture. Lucky her.

"It's not *nothing* I see on your face," Mom snapped, her face red and blotchy with ire. "It's not *nothing* I hear in your voice."

"What is it, then? Since you're the expert on me?"

"You like him."

"I don't."

"You kissed! It was all over the paper."

Instantly she remembered the lush weight of his lips, the way her whole body had contracted with a desire so delicious, so consuming it had seemed painful.

An ache beneath her skin.

It had been unlike any other kiss in her life.

Like her first taste of good wine, sweet and rich. Dangerous.

"Don't lie to yourself, Zoe. That's so dangerous. If you like him, admit it, but pretending you don't is just asking for heartache."

"Okay, fine, let's say I like him. What's wrong with that?"

"Zoe, can't you see what you're doing? This is your pattern. One mistake after another, thinking the second one will fix the first. You rush into situations without thinking."

Zoe felt a cold chill at the top of her spine and sat down on the stool by the counter.

Penny was right.

She did know a thing or two about mistakes.

"I've picked you up after every heartbreak, every disappointment, every situation you thought was going to be so amazing, only to have it fall apart around you."

"I know," she said, numbed by the truth.

"You need to use your head now, not your heart. Your life is about to be harder, in ways you don't even understand, and that man will be gone."

"Not every man is like Dad."

"And you can tell me for sure that Carter O'Neill isn't? That he'd stick around for the birth of a baby that isn't his?"

There was no chance of that, Zoe thought. None at all.

And, despite the magic and the teasing and the zing under her skin when she saw him, she didn't want him around for the birth of her baby, so this whole argument was moot.

"It's just some fun, Mom. That's it."

"It's never just fun," Penny said, shaking her head. "Someone always gets hurt. Always. And I don't want that person to be you, because you've got enough on your plate."

See, Zoe thought, her impulsive nature once again stymied by Mom's rationality. There was nothing her mother said that she could argue with.

Liking him, really liking Carter, was asking for trouble.

"You're so busy with work and getting things ready for the baby, you don't have time to be distracted."

That, too, was true.

"There will be men, in the future, if you want them, but there is only one time in your life like this. One time to devote to your child."

And another one for Mom.

"You know I'm right," Penny said, her case made, Zoe sitting slightly sad over a mess of apples.

"You are," Zoe admitted, taking a piece of apple off the cutting board.

A couple more dates, a few more photographs, and she and Carter were over. They had to be.

MONDAY, CARTER SAID good-night to Larry at the security desk then stepped out into the black-edged purple night. It fit his mood, dark and darker.

This impending moment had been riding him all day. The cherry on top of what had already been a weird day.

His meeting with Lafayette had been successful, but even that victory couldn't chase Zoe out of his thoughts.

Why had he told Zoe his feelings for her weren't businesslike? What idiotic devil had possessed him to say something so stupid? These dates were fake. Arranged.

Zoe had it right—this was business. Nothing else.

And somehow Zoe shook that. Made him wish things were different.

He turned left outside the glass doors and searched the quiet dusk for evil blondes of his bloodline. The night-blooming jasmine battled with the smells of the city street, and he could hear the highway humming in the distance. But right now, right here, all was quiet in his city.

Across the street, in the deepest shadows in the alleyway between a McDonald's and a barbershop, he saw a flash of white, the glowing tip of a cigarette.

And then it was gone.

He paused for a moment, making sure no photographer was following him, then he cut across the street, eager to have this over with. A taxi honked, breezing past, and he ignored it, focused instead on finding his mother and getting rid of her once and for all.

He stepped into the murky darkness of the alley and found her behind a fire escape. Her blond hair was pulled back, her black shirt swallowing the light. Her face was tight, her eyes shuddered.

She was subdued.

And it freaked him out. Put an edge to his anger. He didn't need to battle through one more act, one more false face.

She was never going to be his mother. She was certainly never going to be a friend, but why the hell did everything have to be a game?

"You look like a thief," he said, stopping a good three feet from her. Any closer and he was scared she'd try to touch him and then, with this desire for a fight, he didn't know what he'd do.

"You look like a suit," she said, pointing at him with her cigarette. "I swear you're the only O'Neill to wear a suit who wasn't selling something. Or maybe you are?" She tilted her head. "Lord knows you aren't the first O'Neill to try politics as their scam of choice. Your great-uncle Jasper made a fortune—"

"I'm not like you," he said. "So you can stop trying to tie the family bonds."

She paused as if she was going to say something, but in the end she just took a drag of her cigarette.

"You were wrong," Carter said, cutting to the chase. "The gems aren't in the house and no one has come sneaking around. Margot's in West Palm Beach and unless she travels with a fortune in stolen gems—"

"She doesn't," she sighed, smoke circling her head. "She doesn't have the jewels. I'm guessing she never did."

"How do you know that?" he asked, something about the authority in her tone making him nervous. "What did you do?"

"I had someone break into their hotel room, Carter. What do you think I did? Don't worry," she sighed, watching his face. "The guy was a pro. They don't even know anyone was there. She doesn't have safe-deposit boxes. She doesn't rent a safe in hotels."

"I can't believe you—"

"I honestly thought she had the gems," she said, her laughter sounding angry and sad at the same time and Carter felt as if he'd been dropped in some kind of wormhole. "It would be so like her, making me jump through hoops, chasing my tail all over the damn world while she sat in Bonne Terre laughing."

"I don't think anyone's laughing," Carter said. "Not after you broke into The Manor last summer."

Vanessa dropped her cigarette and ground it out with the toe of a high-heeled foot. "I know. That was a mistake. This whole damn thing has been a mistake."

"Do you have the gems?" he asked, wondering what game she was playing, because he hadn't been dealt the same cards.

She stared at him, her eyes sharp and angry. "Why would I go to all this trouble, Carter?" she asked. "If I had the damn gems."

"To get back into our lives," he said. Even as the words came out of his mouth he realized it wasn't the case. Not for Vanessa. Maybe in books or movies, when the bad guy was really a good guy in the end. But Vanessa was only greedy for money. Never greedy for her children.

Her silence confirmed it.

He blinked as his rage ignited. "Then what the hell was the point of all this? Are we a game to you? A score? Is this…?" Carter could not get his head around what she wanted, why she was here. "Are you playing some kind of angle?"

She tilted her face back and looked up at the

sky. "I'm way on the other side of fifty, broke and alone. I'm out of angles, Carter. I'm done."

Carter laughed before he could help himself. "You've got to be kidding me."

She shook her head, pulling out another cigarette and lighting it. "I'm sorry I bothered you, Carter. I'm sorry I bothered any of you."

She turned as if to leave and Carter felt a jagged slice at his gut, a lightning-quick knife in his chest—his whole body deflating in shock.

"This is it?" he asked. "You come back into my life for nothing? And now you just walk away?"

She paused, smoked half a cigarette in the charged silence. He could hear himself breathing, his heart pounding. "The gems… I thought it was my way out of the game, you know, for good. Otherwise I wouldn't have broken our agreement," she said. "I wouldn't have scared Savannah…and her daughter."

Your granddaughter, he thought, *you can't even say the word.*

"That's it?"

"What more do you want from me, Carter. I'm sorry. For all of it. You want to talk?" she asked, her voice joking, but a light sparking in her eyes. "Get a cup of coffee?"

"Hell no!" he cried. "I want to know why you came back! We had an agreement. I've spent the last ten years away from my brother and sister in

fear of bringing you back to them. Afraid of con-
taminating them with the lies I told!"

"Oh, Carter, it wasn't Federal Court. No one
cares anymore."

"I know what it was, Vanessa! I told the lie and
I sure as hell care!"

She stepped up to him, so close he could smell
her perfume, see the black rim around her iris. She
searched his eyes, his face, and her sudden smile
was sad.

"I'm sorry I made you do that," she said.

He felt fire burning through his veins, inciner-
ating every logical thing he might say. *Sorry?* he
thought. *She was sorry?*

"What about dropping us off with Margot?" His
voice burned, rising up through his throat from
some unknown furnace in his gut.

She shook her head. "Nope. That was the right
thing to do. I'm a pretty crap mother." She watched
him as he stood there, running hot and cold, feeling like his head might explode. "You guys turned
out better without me."

Honesty? Honesty from Vanessa O'Neill. Was
this really happening? Was he making this up?
When he was a kid he used to dream about this
crap—whole nights spent dedicated to the many
ways his mother would tell him that she'd screwed
up.

"You okay?" she asked. Her smile, not sharp,

not cold, not that evil slice across her mouth that held a thousand lies, was soft. Like a mother's.

Not that he really knew what that looked like.

"You've had a bad day," she said. "I saw the paper."

Right. The paper. He pushed away from her, wiping his face. He didn't need the two giant crap piles in his life converging in one giant crap pile.

"It's that girl from the community center, right?" Vanessa asked. "The one I paid." Carter braced himself against the fire escape, the metal cool in his hot hands.

Leave, he told himself, *just leave.*

But he couldn't. Not while she was still talking. It was as if she held a magnet, and as long as she answered his questions, he couldn't walk away.

"She looks about five months pregnant."

He watched her through narrowed eyes, waiting for her to say what had to be on the tip of her tongue, the tip of everyone's tongue, but she was silent.

"I'd never met her before you paid her to get my attention. I'm not the father," he finally snapped.

"I know you're not," she said.

"How?" he asked, "Mother's intuition?"

"I know a first kiss when I see one."

Stupidly, unbelievably, he smiled.

"You like her?" Vanessa asked.

"I am not talking about my love life with you."

He sounded like a defensive teenager and she smiled.

"Ahh, you *do* like her." She took another drag from her cigarette. "It's okay, Carter. You can be happy. You deserve it."

"You're an authority on happy?" he asked.

"Pretty much the other way around," she said. "There's not an inch of unhappy I haven't seen firsthand."

"Is that supposed to make me feel sorry for you?"

"The last thing I expect is for you to feel sorry for me. But if you like this girl, don't run scared. Proud is a lonely way to spend your life."

"You didn't have to let go of us," he said, not even sure if she was talking about her kids, but wanting to say it anyway. "You didn't have to take that money from Margot every month."

She didn't give him an answer, probably didn't have one, and he hated that he wanted one. He was doomed to disappointment when it came to his mother.

"I better go," she said. "We don't want our picture on the front page of the paper now, do we."

Her black shirt blended into the night, the gleam of her blond hair the only indication she was there.

"Where are you going?"

"Nowhere yet," she said.

"I can't have you here, Mom. It's bad for me."

"I know, Carter, and I'm sorry. But there's nothing I can do about that."

"What are you going to do?"

"Don't worry about me, Carter," she said, her voice spooling out from the darkness. "I'll be fine."

And then she was gone.

JIM STAYED IN THE SHADOWS at the top of the alley, holding his breath as Carter walked past, practically breathing smoke and fire. Whatever he and the film noir blonde had been talking about, it hadn't made the golden boy happy.

And that made Jim smile, despite his own frustration. He'd been too far away to hear anything, but Jim would put money on the blond woman being Vanessa O'Neill. Carter's long-lost Mommy.

Conspiracy to sell stolen gems, that had to carry jail time. All Jim needed was to connect a few dots to make sure Carter O'Neill went down.

And he had the perfect way to make sure those dots got connected.

He flipped open his phone and pressed three on his speed dial.

"Yo, Jimmy!" boomed Louis, the photographer Jim used in situations like this O'Neill one. Jim cringed at the nickname, at the stupidity that dripped off this guy's voice. Louis hadn't even graduated community college, but what he did for a living didn't require it. "What's up?"

"Nothing, Louis, I just have a job for you."

"Well, I liked the Deputy Deadbeat Daddy Denied job. Made a nice chunk of change off that sweet picture."

"Good, because it's more of the same."

"Same what?"

Dear God, Jim thought, *save me from the idiots.*

"I need you to follow Zoe Madison, maybe get some friends to do the same."

"Dude, the story is cold. No one gives a shit about the pregnant girl anymore."

"That's not true—"

Louis was silent, having picked a fine time to get wise. "I'll pay you," Jim said.

Louis sighed. "All right, Jimmy, it's your dime. Not sure why you want to spend it on pictures of a dead story."

I'd explain it to you, Jim thought, *but you'd never understand. Leverage* was too big a word for Louis.

CHAPTER SEVEN

"Hands," Zoe yelled over the violins in the Mozart gavotte. "Watch your hands, Sophie."

Frustrated, Zoe circled the pirouetting girl in the room, walking in front of the cracked mirrors over to the stereo in the corner.

She pushed the off button and Sophie and the violins both stopped. These Saturday morning lessons weren't going well.

"When is your audition?" Zoe asked and Sophie blushed, flexing and unflexing her hands.

"January 10."

"Great," Zoe said, walking up to the girl and taking her hands. "That gives us five weeks to get rid of these lobster claws."

"They're that bad?"

"Worse," Zoe said. "Juilliard does not accept lobsters into their dance program."

"You know," Sophie said, her tone going sour and making Zoe want to roll her eyes. She wanted to tell Sophie that Juilliard didn't accept spoiled little girls who used excuses to explain bad technique, either, but she couldn't be too sure of it.

"None of my other teachers have ever said anything about my hands."

Zoe stepped back, lifted her head and looked down her nose the way all of her former choreographers and teachers had stood, a posture that was guaranteed to put dancers in their places. The look was as old as toe shoes, and Zoe found she liked it, liked using it. "Then every other teacher you've had has done you a disservice. You came to me because you want into Juilliard, right?"

Sophie nodded, her jaw tight but her mouth shut.

"Your feet are exquisite," Zoe said, and Sophie perked up. "Your legs are good, not great, but they show lots of promise. Which leaves…"

"My hands," Sophie muttered.

"Five fingers," Zoe said, manipulating the girl's hand into something more elegant than a claw. She extended the girl's arm. "Finish the movement, all the way down your arm into your hand and finally your fingers. Without your fingers, you're leaving the movement incomplete. You're chopping it off at the elbow. Got it?"

Sophie nodded. "I'm trying," she said truthfully, without whining, which was a serious improvement. "I really am."

"I know you are," Zoe said with a slight smile, playing the benevolent teacher to the hilt. "I'll see you tomorrow."

Sophie walked away. Her back was straight and strong, but ballet was a cruel master and the strength it required to be a professional was not found only in the muscles.

"She got a chance?" Phillip asked from behind her, making her jump in surprise.

"Maybe," she sighed, "hard to say just yet." She turned, resigned to this moment. She'd been dodging his calls all week and she couldn't avoid him forever. "I wasn't expecting you."

"I know," he said and handed her a decaf latte and a grease-stained bag.

"Frayley's Beignets?" She couldn't stop her voice from squealing. Thirty-seven years old and she squealed for beignets.

"Salted," Phillip said with a face. "Just how you like them."

She popped a hot grease ball into her mouth and it exploded with salt and sweetness. Why wasn't the whole world eating beignets this way?

"So, why don't you tell me why you're avoiding me?"

"I haven't—"

"Cut the crap, Zoe. What's going on?"

Phillip crossed his arms over a thin cashmere sweater that did fabulous things for both his eyes and his chest.

"Not much," she hedged, and he snorted.

"Fine," she said, "I went to the ballet with Carter O'Neill."

"I saw the picture," he said, his eyebrows raised. "You went to the ballet wearing a tablecloth from an Italian restaurant."

"It was all I had," she said, regretting her decision not to care what she looked like Wednesday night. Especially since the photograph was all over the paper.

"How was the ballet?" he asked.

"Gorgeous," she answered truthfully. But the rest of the night, sitting beside Carter, awkwardly trying not to hit each other with elbows and knees, was terrible.

And after the photo and all that nonsense, there'd been a strange moment when, against all her better judgment, she'd been about to ask him to go for coffee. It had seemed as if he'd been about to do the same, and they'd laughed like teenagers.

But then, that cold mask had settled over his face, and Carter had said good-night and left.

And she'd watched him go, feeling foolish.

"So, you're dating Carter O'Neill?" Phillip asked.

"We're just friends."

"Bullshit, Zoe. There's a photographer outside," he said, pointing toward the door. "I don't think photographers are following O'Neill's other friends."

She put another beignet in her mouth. That photographer had been following her since Tuesday morning, and she didn't understand why.

"And some reporter called me," Phillip said. "Wanted to know all about you and the mayor pro tem."

She twisted to look at him. Carter had been right. "What did you say?"

"That it was none of his business," he said with a shrug. "If my best friend has found love with a suit that doesn't mind her dressing in tablecloths, more power to her."

She laughed, but it was greasy with guilt. She stepped away across the small dark studio toward the makeshift stage, next to the wall of cracked and broken mirrors. She sat her pregnant self down next to the stereo and put the brown bag in her lap where the beignets nestled together like eggs in a nest.

Unable to pretend to her best friend that all was right in her world, she let the whole story spill out.

"So you and Carter aren't real?" he asked when she was done, and she shook her head. "It's all a press stunt?"

"I'm calling it public service," she said.

"Oh, honey," Phillip said, putting his arm around her and hugging her tight. "I hated feeling left in the dark, and I'm pretty pissed you've kept it a secret, but I was beginning to be happy with the idea that you'd found someone."

She pulled away from Phillip, looking up into his warm brown eyes. She remembered when she used to love him, before they'd both understood that he was gay. They'd taken dance classes together for years, and she often wondered if she'd have stuck with dance for as long as she had if it hadn't been for him.

"I'm lonely," she said, cupping his cheek. "But I'm not desperate to bring a man into my life."

"What about sex?"

"Sex?" she asked. "Isn't that a chair from IKEA?"

"That bad, huh?"

"You have no idea," she groaned, slumping against him.

"It's only been five months," Phillip laughed, rubbing her belly.

Oops, she thought. She really needed to be more careful if she didn't want to end up explaining the father of her baby. Phillip wasn't dumb—he'd catch on sooner or later.

"Feels like forever," she said.

"Six months is only the beginning of a dry spell," he said. "A year is officially a drought. More than two years and you have a climate change situation."

Phillip made a joke of it, but that's what Phillip

did. He laughed off the tough stuff—his father leaving, his family on welfare, having to give up dance. He was more handsome than anyone needed to be, so no one ever credited him with much depth.

"How long has it been?" she asked, the pain lacing his joke so obvious it filled the room.

"One year, one month, two weeks, three days."

"He's—"

"Getting better." Phillip's optimism was sincere. It had been just over a year since his partner, Ben, had been in a car accident that had totally crushed his hips, and it seemed as though corners were being turned every day. He'd gone back to work last month at his law firm as a consultant for the state government. "He's out of the wheelchair most of the day now. He only uses it at night when he's tired. And yesterday—" Phillip's eyes got big "—Ben got a boner!"

"What?"

"We were in the shower," Phillip said. "Soaping each other up and suddenly, there it was!"

"What did you do?"

Phillip's laughter was so bright and beautiful it brought tears to Zoe's eyes. "What do you think I did?" Phillip asked. "I dropped to my knees and got reacquainted."

She laughed so hard the baby did somersaults. "You're amazing, you know that?"

Phillip took a sip of her latte. "It's Ben that's amazing," he said. "I swear to God, every day…" He trailed off and shook his head. "Best man in a suit I've ever known."

"Well, I think the suit part gets negated by the fact that he dressed up like Dolly Parton on the weekends."

"He does look good in sequins," Phillip said with a smile that spoke of such love she had to look away, choked up.

She wasn't lonely, not really. But she wanted to feel what Phillip felt for Ben.

And there was the sex. Sex sometime in the future would be nice.

But not with Carter.

No matter how much her body might want it, her head and heart were voting no.

"Honey?" he said, jostling her. "A boner is nothing to cry about."

"I know." She smiled, waving her hands in an attempt to laugh off the spikes of emotion that were making her do crazy things. Want crazy things. "It's the hormones."

"Do you…like Carter?" Phillip asked, leaning to look into her eyes.

"Sure," she said, pretending to be casual.

"What's he like?"

Funny. Sad, a little. Warmer than he thinks. More passionate than anyone knows. Driven. Single-minded. Sometimes cold. Secretive. Confusing in about a hundred different ways.

"Surprising," she finally said. "But not for me, so let's stop talking about him."

The two of them sat in a nice silence, like a warm puddle of sunshine. She ate some salty beignets and decided to put voice to the idea she'd had while tossing and turning in bed the other night.

"You used to take hip-hop classes, right?"

"Like a million years ago," he said. But she knew Phillip was being modest. He'd been as passionate about dance as she had, but Phillip was one of five kids and his mom hadn't been able to sacrifice everything the way Zoe's mom had. After Phillip's dad had left, when it had come down to dance class or paying the electric bill—the electric bill got paid.

"You said you were taking classes again a few years ago."

"I did. I do."

She turned to him, eyes wide. "Why didn't you tell me?"

"It's only one class a week. You don't tell me everything."

"Touché," she said, but secretly she was thrilled. This idea was actually doable.

"What about break dancing—"

"That I did in the eighties?" he asked with a laugh. "When I was ten?"

"But you were good."

He pursed his lips. "I *was* good, wasn't I?"

"I was thinking about offering a free class to teenagers after school. Hip-hop, maybe some jazz. Break dancing."

He swiveled and stared at her. "Where did this come from?"

Carter, she thought, remembering the fire in his eyes.

But instead of telling her best friend the truth, she shrugged, glancing down at a grease stain that looked like a pair of lips. "Just an idea."

"It's a good one," he said, and she knew he was remembering the days when a free dance class might have changed his life. It was why she'd asked him—he had more in common with these kids than she did, and without commonality, this idea was useless.

"I can't pay you."

"I don't need to get paid. I'll help, but I'm no expert." He glanced over her head to the mirror. He popped and locked his arms, flipped up his collar, did a wave. "Still got it, though."

She put her arms around the man in her life and gave him a big hug. "You definitely got it."

CARTER WASN'T SURE WHAT he was doing here.

He didn't even like soul food.

Yet here he was, at seven o'clock on Sunday night, outside…he squinted into the shadows at the faded sign over the door. Mama's. A soul food place called Mama's.

No wonder Zoe loves this place, he thought. It was authentic, real and true, like her. Even the air outside the place smelled good enough to eat. The flame of warmth that sparked to life when he even thought her name made him nervous. He wasn't supposed to care.

But now he was thinking about soul food. Because of her.

Ever since the ballet on Wednesday, he'd been thinking about her more and more. Four days and it felt so much longer.

"This is ridiculous," he muttered.

He should have just called her, because that's what he really wanted to do. Plan another fake date, so he could see her again.

But there was no need. After the ballet and the picture in the paper, his poll numbers had stopped dipping.

So if he called her, it would be for him alone. Strictly personal.

"In or out, buddy?" a guy asked, standing behind him. Carter didn't move and the guy stepped around him, yanking open the door. Delicious smells and warmth and light spilled out the door then vanished, and Carter stood again in the darkness outside.

Always outside.

Carter scoffed at his own melodrama. *In or out, Carter?* he thought. He went in.

The menu was printed on a chalkboard over the counter and on sticky plastic menus. Even the floor was sticky and Carter had to wonder how much they bribed public health in order to stay open.

"Carter?"

The voice was hers and he jumped, spinning around as if he'd been caught doing something illegal.

Zoe's smile was bright, luminous even, and then as he watched, she controlled it. Tamed it and put it back under wraps. But that first smile...oh, that first smile told him a lot.

"What are you doing here?" she asked, switching her bag from one shoulder to the other. She looked tired and he reached for the bag.

"Here, let me—"

She put up a little protest, but he took the bag from her, swinging the embroidered sack over his shoulder.

"What's in here?" he asked, astonished at its weight.

"Hard to say," she said with a weary smile. "I need to clean it out."

You need to take it easy, he thought but didn't say. It wasn't his place. Their relationship was business, and it looked as if it was coming to an end.

Besides, he was in enough trouble with Blackwell and his mother in the same city. He didn't need to complicate things with Zoe.

And everything about Zoe was a complication.

But he still wanted her, he still wanted to brush back her hair and kiss her pink lips.

Wednesday night, he'd watched her more than the ballet. He'd watched her eyes gleam, her lips part with smiles and sighs. Her fingers dancing across her lap. He'd felt her muscles tense when the ballerina leaped.

He'd felt, it seemed, her spirit—buoyant and happy.

Her joy had been contagious, and his stark life, his strict existence, had soaked up that joy like a sponge.

"Are you here because of the photographers?" she asked.

"What photographers?" he asked, looking out the small front window onto the street.

"The ones still following me."

His mouth dropped open for a second. "I had no idea. No one is following me."

"Lucky you. It's mostly one guy and his heart doesn't seem to be into it."

"How are you feeling?" he asked.

"Like a whale. On my good days. But you don't want to hear about my swollen ankles."

"Sure I do," he said. And he meant it.

She watched him, her eyes measuring his sincerity, as if she were trying to find his angle. His motives for caring.

The moment got small and tight; it was the night of the ballet all over again. The air between them was cluttered with too many emotions: wariness, genuine respect and a heaping dose of lust. At least on his part. And he had the sinking suspicion that he was alone with that.

But then she cleared her throat, her eyes darting away, and the moment shattered.

Apparently his sincerity was unconvincing.

"I have a doctor's appointment on Tuesday, and I'm sure the whale feelings are par for the course. The real question is, what are you doing here? I thought you didn't like soul food."

"Someone recommended this place to me," he said and her smile was quick. A flash, like the memory of the one kiss they shared, and then it was gone. "Truth is, I've never had any. I mean, other than what my grandmother cooked and I imagine that was pretty tame compared to..." He gestured toward the giant black woman behind the cash register, who had to be ninety if she was a day.

"Mama is the best," Zoe said and the woman behind the cash—Mama, Carter deduced—broke into a wide warm smile.

"Hi, sugar," she said and Zoe let herself get pulled into a monstrous hug. It looked good; Carter couldn't lie. He was tired and worn-out, and getting folded into that giant hug seemed like a pretty good way to spend a few seconds.

"This is Carter," Zoe said, turning to introduce Carter.

"I know who he is," Mama said, and as she tucked her arms up under her shelf of breasts Carter prepared himself for more deadbeat daddy stuff.

"Mama," Zoe whispered. "He's not the father."

"Oh, any fool could see that," Mama said. "Not sure what's going on there, but Mr. O'Neill, you got my vote if you gonna be running for mayor. We need to be cleaning up these communities, like you been trying to do."

Carter smiled, pleased and relieved. Zoe looked stunned, as if shocked that anyone believed in his message.

"Thank you, Ma'am."

"Call me Mama. Now, what you two having?"

"I'll have what she's having," he said.

Zoe ordered catfish and greens, and she reached for her bag to pay, but he put down a twenty.

"Eat with me," he said, the words popping out of his mouth, inspired by the strain around her eyes and the weary slouch to her shoulders.

She seemed unsure. As if saying yes might change their arrangement.

"It's just dinner," he said, feeling oddly slighted.

She shook her head. "It's not, Carter," she said, so forthright and honest it shook him. "Not for me. I like you. I need to go with my head on this one. And my head says dinner would be a mistake."

"When have you ever gone with your head, Zoe?" He didn't know much about her, but that she lived through her heart was obvious to the world.

"That's the problem," she said. "That's always the problem."

"Then how about coffee," he said. "Thursday?"

"More reputation repair work?"

If that's all he could get.

You're pathetic, he told himself, but himself wasn't listening.

"Yes," he said. "We can meet at the coffee shop outside city hall."

Mama slid big takeaway boxes onto the counter.

"Here y'all are," she said. "Have at it."

Zoe took her bag, swinging it up over her shoulder, and then took the food.

"Zoe," he said. "Let me help."

"I'm fine," she said. "Really."

She wasn't going to let him help. She wasn't going to eat with him. She was shutting him right out.

Just business.

She'd told him—he shouldn't be so hurt or surprised. But he was.

"Well—" her smile was sharp and false, a knife through his stomach "—I guess…I'll see you on Thursday."

"Sure," he said.

And she was gone.

TWENTY MINUTES LATER, Zoe climbed the stairs to her loft, feeling harried and fat and more pregnant than any one woman should. Her head hurt as though she had an emotional hangover from seeing Carter. He'd looked faded, somehow, and she'd wanted to ask him what was wrong. She wanted to ask him about his day, tell him about hers. About the two-year-old in her toddler class who'd told the whole room about peeing in the potty.

But she'd done the right thing, saying no to dinner. She was proud of herself. If only proud gave her the same warm tingles that Carter did.

Distracted by her mixed emotions, she nearly

collided with a man standing right in front of her door.

"Ohmygod," she yelped, leaping back and bumping into the wall. Her heart thundered so hard against her chest she saw stars. "Who the hell are you?"

"I'm so sorry," the man said, holding his hands out. He seemed contrite, but she'd been bombarded by people who weren't what they seemed these days. "I really am, I didn't mean to scare you."

The guy had kind of a puppy dog face, soft cheeks and heavy eyes. Brown hair that was a little shaggy.

The kind of guy that shocked neighbors said seemed so nice, so unassuming, after all the dead bodies were found in his apartment.

She slipped her hand into her bag for the Mace attached to her key ring. She was a woman alone in the world—she wasn't a fool.

"What do you want?" she asked.

"Not to get sprayed with Mace," he said, nodding down to the hand in her bag. His smile was lopsided and sweet, and it almost made her forget that he'd somehow broken into her building and had been lying in wait for her.

He reached for his pocket and she whipped her Mace up and out of the bag. "I'm getting my ID," he said. "That's all."

"My neighbors are really nosy," she said in

warning. "One peep out of me and all these doors will open."

She didn't say that all her neighbors were about eighty years old and he could overpower them with one hand.

"I'm a reporter. My name is Jim Blackwell."

Now she recognized him. He was the reporter with the cell phone camera in that meeting. He was the reason she was in the papers.

"I know who you are," she snapped. "And if you don't want to get maced on principle, then you've got about five seconds to get the hell out of here."

"Hear me out—"

"Five. Four."

"The photographers following you have gotten out of hand," he said. "And I'm here to give you a chance to clear the air. I swear, once you do that, the photographers will leave you alone."

Alone? Alone was good. Alone was heaven.

"You stopped counting, so can I assume you're interested?"

"You can," she said, lowering the Mace.

"Aren't you usually a city hall writer?" she asked. "The identity of my baby's father seems a little beneath you. Because it's not Carter O'Neill."

"I was pretty sure." His smirk made her skin crawl.

"So...there's not much else to talk about."

"You could talk about Carter," he said, and something in his voice, the electric expectation on his face, made her nervous.

"What do you mean?"

"Look, I know you don't have insurance and having a baby is expensive. I'd be happy to pay you—"

"For what exactly?"

"For…" He sighed. "I don't know, whatever you might find out about Carter. About his family. His mother."

She nearly dropped her bag.

"Are you asking me to spy for you?"

"I'm asking you to do your civic duty."

She laughed; she couldn't help it. "I'm sorry. But, wow, that's…ah…that's a stretch. Civic duty?"

"Look, Carter O'Neill is up to no good. His whole family is involved with this gem theft—"

"He's a good guy," she said, not entirely sure why she needed to defend Carter. Maybe because he defended her to the photographers the night of their date. Or maybe because he looked so alone inside Mama's. Or maybe because she was a total sucker. "I mean as far as city officials go, he wants to help—"

"Himself," Jim said, his puppy dog eyes growing razor sharp.

Everything in Zoe recoiled, shrinking away

from the man, and he must have sensed it because he stepped away.

"I'm sorry I scared you," he said, that charming half smile back on his lips. He nodded down to the card in her fingers. "If you want all this to end, just give me a call. I'm sure you don't want it to get worse."

The threat hung in the air like a bad smell and she watched him wave and walk away. That man was a snake, and as bad as her life was right now, she wasn't going to make it worse by lying down with snakes.

CHAPTER EIGHT

"THE MAYOR WOULD LIKE to see you," Gloria, Carter's receptionist, said as Carter stormed past her desk early Wednesday morning.

"He's in already?" he asked, wishing he'd had a bit more time for damage control this morning before meeting with Bill. On the front page of today's paper, Jim Blackwell had done his best to make the donation from Lafayette Corp. seem like the administration was selling its soul. And Carter was the devil sealing the deal.

"He's been here since seven," Gloria whispered. "His assistant said he's ticked with a capital *t*."

"Great," Carter muttered. He tossed his raincoat and briefcase across the small couch inside his door and headed back out toward the office at the end of the hallway.

"Good luck," Gloria called out after him.

"Thanks," he muttered. He was going to need it.

Julie, the Mayor's assistant, winced when she saw him. "Go on in. He's expecting you," she said.

He took a deep breath outside the door, feeling as if he was about to face a firing squad.

"Mayor?" he asked, stepping into the elegant inner office. The desk, the shelves that lined all the walls, were made of thick, polished oak and the sun bounced off them and made the whole room glow with a warm light.

The river and the highway flowed past his windows.

It was a beautiful room to be fired in, if it came to that.

"Morning, Carter," Bill said, spinning in his chair to face him. In the early-morning light, the mayor looked his age—which was closer to seventy than anyone wanted to admit.

But his eyes were still sharp and his mind the sharpest this city had seen. He'd served as mayor for two terms in the eighties and had run again after the Marcuzzi administration, in an effort to pull the city back from the brink. Now, he was a year away from the end of his term.

"Sir, I assume you want to talk about the article regarding the Lafayette deal."

Bill flipped over the front page of the paper spread across his giant desk. "Jim Blackwell is riding you hard these days, Carter."

"I know," Carter said. "But the deal is clean. Lafayette is clean."

"I know, son," he said with a sigh and a small

smile. He stood, his thin body outlined by the sun like a halo. "I know. You know. Eric knows. The city knows. There are always going to be naysayers. Always going to be articles. It's the way it is."

"So…?" Carter tried to find a point in this.

"I'm leaving after this term. I'm done. Too old for this nonsense."

He'd known as much, but the words had never been said out loud. "The city will miss you," he said, and Bill laughed.

"You're a politician all the way down to your underwear." Bill eyed him shrewdly and Carter felt the need to tip his head back and puff out his chest like the troops in front of Patton. "I'd endorse you for the Democratic ticket in the primary, and lord knows the Republicans haven't got anyone who will cause you trouble. But you haven't announced your position, and I'm wondering why?"

I might not be right for the job, he thought, the words beating at his lips, words that had never seen the light of day before. And they never would have seen the light of day—ever—if it weren't for this perfect storm of his mother being back in his life and Jim Blackwell being around to witness it.

"Carter?" Bill asked, looking into Carter's eyes. Carter found the scrutiny uncomfortable—found any scrutiny uncomfortable, and he was tired of being uncomfortable in his own skin.

"I'm worried about my family," Carter blurted.

"Ah, yes, your disreputable family tree."

"Disreputable." Understatement of the year.

"Everyone's got secrets, son. Hell, my father had a boyfriend, and in the eighties, that was a huge liability. But right now, your family is the least of your worries."

"What do you mean?"

"You're good for this town," Bill said, and the compliment filled Carter with pride. "No doubt about it, but right now—you'd be a shit mayor."

Carter's mouth fell open.

"The Lafayette deal is a good piece of work. And the article in the paper is just an article in the paper—there will be millions of them. But this—" he snapped open the paper to the back inside page and held it up to Carter "—is going to be the end of you."

Carter was sucker punched. Gut shot.

"Holy…" he breathed, taking the paper from the mayor. Zoe stared up at him from a black-and-white picture in the local section. The sign for a free clinic was in the background—she'd clearly been ambushed coming out of her doctor's appointment yesterday.

The look on her face was pure panic. Pure fear.

She was scared and it was his fault.

"I understand that this woman was supposed to

help your public image," Bill said, "after all that Deadbeat Daddy nonsense."

"She was. I mean, she is."

"If you want to be mayor, it's time to act like it. *No comment* isn't working anymore."

Carter nodded and folded the paper, hiding Zoe's face because he couldn't take it.

"I'll take care of this," Carter said.

"When you walked into my office two years ago, I had you pegged as a fighter. But the last few months you've been turning yourself into a politician, which is too bad, because politicians ruined this city. We need someone who will fight for what they want and for what is right."

What I want, Carter thought. *Fight for what I want.* It was a foreign concept, but he was tired of lying back and waiting for his family to take away the things he wanted.

He wanted to be mayor and he wanted Zoe.

He was ready to fight.

CARTER STORMED BACK TO his office, a whirlwind of purpose finally forcing him into action. If he wanted to be mayor, he needed to fight for it.

It was time for him to choose his own fate, stop being dictated to by his family. By the mistakes they made.

"Everything okay?" Gloria asked, half standing from behind her desk as he strode by.

"Great," he said and, surprisingly, he meant it. Dormant action burned in him, waiting to get out. "Get me Lafayette Corp. on the phone."

"You bet."

He kicked the door shut behind him and checked his watch; only quarter to eight, too early to call Zoe. He didn't want to start her day with a phone call about this garbage.

That was assuming Zoe would even take his call. He'd been tempted to call her over a dozen times since Sunday night at Mama's, but had resisted each time. Now, after this incident outside the doctor's, who knew if she'd ever want to talk to him again.

He took the folded paper out from under his arm and smoothed it out across his desk and felt his rib cage shrink.

The fear in Zoe's eyes made him sick to his stomach. The way she had her hands crossed across her belly as if to protect the baby made him want to murder someone.

She looked trapped. Scared.

There wasn't a story attached, just a caption: Mayor Pro Tem's Mistress Uses Free Clinic. But Carter knew who was behind all this continued interest in Zoe—Jim Blackwell. It had to be. No one but him would still care.

Zoe and Carter were an ice-cold story.

Suddenly, despite the fact that Zoe had been the

one to stand up on that chair, Carter felt wholly responsible for that look on her lovely face.

This had to change. Right now.

The intercom buzzed and he punched the button.

"Janet from Lafayette Corp. on line three."

"Got it," he said and put the phone on speaker.

"Hi, Janet," he said, sitting back in his chair.

"Well, hello there, Mr. O'Neill. What can I do for you?"

He smiled at the woman's Southern peach accent. Janet ran that office like it was D-day every day, but she never broke a sweat. "I need a favor."

"I specialize in favors."

He laughed, feeling better every moment. He had control again and control felt good. Right. "I know you do. Can you send an invitation to that casino fundraiser you're throwing on Saturday to Jim Blackwell at the *Gazette?*"

"I don't think so, Mr. O'Neill. This morning's article in the paper didn't make him any friends around here."

"Here neither, Janet, trust me. But I want him to see there's nothing to hide. He can ask all the questions he has, make all the accusations he wants in plain view."

"Ah—you're keeping your friends close but your enemies closer?"

"Now you're quoting *The Godfather,* Janet?"

he asked. "Is there any way I can get you to come work for me?"

Janet laughed. "No sir, but maybe we could get you to come work for us."

"Not likely, Janet. Sorry."

"Well, it's worth a shot. I'll send an invite out right now."

"Thank you," he said and hung up.

He dialed the *Gazette* himself and routed by machine to Blackwell's voice mail.

"Stop harassing innocent women, Blackwell," he said. "Makes you look desperate. You have questions? Want to talk? Fine. I'll talk. Call my office."

He hung up, and riding a serious upswing in adrenaline, he dialed Zoe's number.

"Hello?" A woman answered on the second ring, but it wasn't Zoe.

"Hi," he said. "I'm looking for Zoe."

"Who is calling?"

"Carter O'N—"

He jerked the phone away from his ear, but he could still hear the blistering tirade loud and clear. "Ma'am," he said when she stopped to catch her breath. "Ma'am—"

"Don't you *ma'am* me, boy," she said and Carter blinked. Only Margot called him *boy,* and he guessed she was the only one with the right. "This is Penny, Zoe's mother, and I have spent the last twelve hours trying to comfort a hysterical pregnant woman."

Guilt squeezed his brain. "I just want to talk to her."

"Haven't you done enough?" she asked, and the truth felt like stepping into an ice bath.

I'm making it right, he thought, resolve a bright light in his chest.

"I'm sorry," he said. "But I think after today the press will stay away from her."

"Bully for you, Carter O'Neill. If it weren't for you they would never have been following her in the first place."

Carter bit his tongue against the need to remind her about Zoe standing up on a chair accusing him of being the father of her baby, but he knew a protective mama when he was forced to talk to her.

"Penny, if you could please tell her I'm on the phone so that she can decide whether or not to talk to me."

"Her decision would be no if she was here, but she's not."

"Where is she?"

"Working. Trying to make an honest living."

"Jimmie Simpson?" he asked, knowing she worked at several community centers around the city.

"Figure it out yourself, smart man," she said then hung up.

Carter stood, stretching his neck like a boxer going back in the ring for another round.

Suddenly, his office felt too small, the air too stale. Instead of asking Gloria to make another call he decided to take a walk.

But before he left, he called Amanda.

"Let's get a press conference set up," he said.

"Why?"

"I want to announce I'm running for mayor."

"Before Christmas?"

"Yep."

"Well, that's more like the Carter I know. I'm on it."

He disconnected, feeling better than he had in months.

He left his office and headed down two floors to the parks and rec department in the hopes he could convince someone there to break a few HR rules and tell him where Zoe was teaching today.

Because now he had a reason to see her, and nothing was going to stop him.

"THREE IS BETTER THAN ONE," Zoe said, trying to force optimism upon her and Phillip, but Phillip wasn't having any of it.

It was their first free Wednesday after-school class, and things weren't quite starting the way she'd hoped.

"Well, that one's just here for the snack," he

said, pointing to a six-foot teenager in the corner doing his best to eat the whole bag of chips she'd left out. "I told you, you shouldn't have said there were snacks."

"Then we only would have had two people," she said.

One teenager was here for the snacks, another had clearly been dragged here by her grandmother, and now, said grandmother was sitting in front of the doors, a knitting barricade.

But the third one was a young girl who was working some booty-shaking moves in the mirror. Not much talent, but lots and lots of enthusiasm.

"We can work with that," she said. "I mean lots of enthusiasm is better than a little talent, right?"

Phillip didn't answer; his eyes were on her face. She knew what he saw, the dark circles under her eyes and the strain around her mouth.

"You should take a break," he said. "After the paper this morning—"

"I'm fine," she said, though prickles of adrenaline still fluttered over her skin. Being ambushed yesterday coming out of the clinic had scared her nearly to death, and the photograph this morning had made her sick to her stomach.

"You don't have to be so tough."

"Yes," she said, patting his cheek. "I do."

The front door opened and much to her shock, Carter walked in.

Carter, with his tie tugged loose and his shirt-sleeves rolled up, revealing the tanned strength of his forearms.

Just like at Mama's, just like every time she saw him, her body rebelled against her. Her skin went hot, her heart cold. Her hands curled into fists and the knot—the knot deep in her belly that had been turning tighter and tighter in the nights and lonely days—loosened in a great rush that made her dizzy with sudden want.

Phillip stepped toward Carter, his face intent, and Zoe knew her friend was about to give Carter a piece of his mind, so she put up her hand. She could fight her own battles.

"It's not his fault," she said.

"You gotta end this thing with him," Phillip said. "It's getting ridiculous."

"I agree," she said. She'd decided this morning that whatever debt she owed Carter was repaid. Her life didn't need this drama. Though her head was making the decisions, her heart was getting kicked around, and it was time to get out of the line of fire. "Now, go drag those kids away from the snacks and teach them some dance."

"Okay," he said giving her a quick kiss on the cheek. "Shout if you need me."

She caught Carter's eye and his long legs ate the distance between them. Something was different about him today. An inner fire had been lit.

And it was exciting.

She tamped down her reaction to that excitement, ignored the leap in her blood.

"What are you doing here?" she asked when he was within talking distance.

"I wanted to make sure you were okay," he said.

"You should check the papers," she said, making a stab at a joke.

"Zoe," he sighed, and his voice carried a heavy apology.

She shook her head. "Forget it," she said. "I'm fine. It's just a picture."

"Zoe, I—" Suddenly the look on his face was raw and she saw that he wasn't just here for her. Out of pity. There was a storm in his eyes, pain on his face. "God, Zoe, I'm so sorry about how this has turned out."

"Blackwell is really after you," she said, though she didn't tell Carter about Blackwell's visit to her loft on Sunday night.

"I know. I'm going to take care of it," he promised her.

"Can we...can we just be done?" she asked, her stomach hurting. It was hard to look in his eyes. This wasn't a breakup; there was nothing to break up. It was the end of an agreement.

It shouldn't feel so bad.

"I mean, I know I made things hard for you

when I stood up on that chair, and if you need me, I can still go on dates…or whatever. But if there's a chance you don't need me, and your political career is no longer in trouble, can we…stop?"

Silently, he stepped closer, and she felt him, his presence like a touch on her skin even though inches still separated them.

"Is that what you really want?" he asked, and the heat from his body made her melt.

What I want? she thought. Oddly enough, what she wanted was to curl up against that man and sleep for about ten days. And then she wanted to have sex with him for another ten.

But life without Carter would be simpler.

And right now, she needed simple.

"That's what I want," she said. The second the words were out, she wanted to gobble them back up.

He nodded once, his blue eyes piercing her, holding her still for his scrutiny, and it was unbearable. She couldn't tell what he was thinking, whether he had any reaction at all to her ending the arrangement.

There was some commotion at the snack table, and both Zoe and Carter turned to watch Phillip try to wrestle the bag of chips away from the giant while Grandma's little prisoner was texting on her phone and enthusiastic girl was channeling Beyoncé.

His chuckle ran over her skin, giving her goose bumps. "What exactly are you doing here?" he asked.

She felt the blush climb up her neck across her face. *Following your lead,* she thought, *putting your words to action.*

"It's…ah…a free dance class for kids in East Brookstown."

East Brookstown being one of the roughest neighborhoods in Baton Rouge.

She felt Carter's eyes on her and she tried not to turn and face him, but in the end she couldn't help it. It was as if he tipped the room, the whole world, and everything in her wanted to run downhill to be close to him.

His gaze was warm, assessing, and it made her open her mouth and just babble.

"As you can see we're just starting. I didn't have a chance to truly spread the word and the parks and rec department said that next session they'd be able to put some push behind it, but for now it's just flyers and word of mouth. But—"

"It's amazing," he said, which was a stretch. Across the room, Phillip had barely managed to arrange the three kids in a line in front of the mirror. "The Zoe Madison Dance Academy."

It was ridiculous. She knew that but, somehow, at this moment, Carter seemed so lonely. Or alone. Watching this clumsy dance program inspired by him, but seeming removed from it. From everything. But eager for it. Hungry for it.

It was as if he were locked deep under his skin, trying hard to reach out.

"You inspired me," she blurted. "That night at Bola. What you said about plugging kids into things that interested them."

"I'm glad. A dance class is an excellent idea," he murmured, then he shook his head, as if forcing himself to be honest. "I'm moved, actually. It's not often I get to see the immediate result of something I care about. I swear, most days I sit on the phone trying to change the city and the real work, the real change, is happening right here."

She stared at him, trying to think of rocks and dams, fortresses and castles, things that stood firm. Unmoved.

"I guess, maybe I'm jealous," he said, and she felt all the firm ground beneath her resolve turn to quicksand.

"Well," she joked, "if you know how to break dance…"

He laughed, breaking the unbearable tension between them, and she breathed a sigh of relief. "If it was skateboarding, I might be able to help you."

"What?" she cried.

"I was a skateboarder—"

"Shut up."

"It's that hard to believe?"

"Yes!" she cried. "It is!"

"Well." He looked chagrined and totally adorable. She wanted to wrap her arms around him and smooth back his mussed hair. "I wasn't very good, really. My brother, though—" his smile was distant and fond, and she held her breath, waiting for him to reveal something else, some small glimpse into his life "—he had the talent."

"What's his name?" she asked, and wanted to hit herself. *Don't care! You're not supposed to care!*

"Tyler. Ty. He was one of those guys who was good at everything he did."

"And you're so different?"

He stared at her for a long time and she realized, her heart breaking, that he truly didn't see himself the way she did. The way the world did.

"Anyway," he said, changing the subject. "What you're doing here is great. If you need help with anything. Funding or…" He paused, and his eyes began to glow with a bright speculative light that made her nervous but giddy at the same time, as if he was looking at her as a teammate. A friend. "What are you doing on Saturday?"

"Nothing that would get my picture in the paper," she said.

"I don't blame you," he said. "But I got the funding for the Glenview Community Center—"

"Congratulations!" she cheered. "That's great, Carter. You must feel so good."

He opened and shut his mouth like a beached fish, as if unsure how to respond, and then he laughed a little. *Poor guy,* she thought, *you're so uncomfortable with praise.*

"It does," he said. "It feels really good. But the money comes from a local company—Lafayette Corp."

"I've seen their signs," she said, trying to remember where.

"Construction," he said. "They've been a big part of cleaning up and rebuilding the state in the past few years."

"Right business at the right time," she said, unable to hide the darkness from her voice. It felt like the whole state was falling prey to modern-day carpetbaggers.

"It's not like that, honestly. I've checked these guys out. They're working as green as possible, they've funded half the Habitat for Humanity programs in the parish. Believe it or not, they're the good guys. They're throwing this fundraiser on Saturday—"

"What does that have to do with me?" she asked.

"I don't know, Zoe—they're giving away money to community-based organizations. What do you think it has to do with you?"

Her academy. Explosions went off in her head. Her dream for the academy could actually get off the ground. Now. Not ten years from now, not in that hazy future she always talked about, but right now. As soon as Saturday.

"You don't have to go as my date," he said, his voice cool, his face distant. "I'll get you on the guest list. You can just show up. Ignore me if you want. It's at the Hilton at 8 p.m. It's a Casino night, so sort of formal. I hear there's going to be a chocolate cake made in the shape of a house—"

"You had me at chocolate."

"You'll come?" he asked, his eyes sparkling, that cool facade cracking.

He baffled her, tied her in knots. The way he ran hot and cold might have been exciting to her once upon a time, but now it just made her feel foolish and weary.

But she'd be a fool not to go to the fundraiser. These kinds of chances didn't come around every day, and if she was serious about her future and the future of her academy, these were the chances she needed.

"I'll be there," she said.

"Great!" he said, and he squeezed her hand before leaving.

She watched his wide, strong back detour around Barricade Grandma, and she shook out her hand, trying to clear the goose bumps his touch had left behind.

For all her conviction that going to the fund-raiser was the right thing, it felt scary. Out of her depth.

And it wasn't just that she had nothing to wear, or that she was asking for money for a fledgling idea. It was because Carter, without the cool distance of the business agreement between them, was dangerous.

CHAPTER NINE

SATURDAY NIGHT, CARTER was running late and the party was already in full swing. Walking in through the front doors, he was hit by a wall of sound and heat, a hot wave of perfume mixed with champagne. The two blackjack tables, a poker table and the roulette were moving at full speed with people lined up around them three deep.

A success, he thought, pride and excitement surging through him.

The Glenview albatross was off from around his neck.

He tugged at the white sleeve of his shirt, pulling it past the black edge of his tux. The cuff links, simple silver disks his grandmother had given him on his graduation from law school, were slick under his fingers.

They were usually a pleasant reminder of his childhood, of poker games in Margot's bedroom, arguing with his brother and making his sister giggle, eating cold slices of sugar pie and learning how to count cards and stack the deck.

But here, on the precipice of a chance for a new

life, they reminded him of everything he was and tried to forget.

He caged the nostalgia and regret, locked it up and shoved it a million miles beneath his tux, beneath his desires for this city, beneath his craving to see Zoe here tonight.

It had been hard to accept her terminating their arrangement, a shock after deciding he was going to fight for her. But he couldn't ignore her wishes, and one look in her eyes told him that the photographer and Jim Blackwell were simply too much to ask her to take on.

But she was coming tonight and once he dealt with Blackwell, maybe, just maybe, he could convince her to try again with him. For real this time.

Carter caught sight of Amanda, elegant in a black gown, working Eric Lafayette, and he imagined Eric was working her right back. There had been more than a little sizzle when they'd met yesterday.

"Hello, Carter."

Carter turned to find Jim Blackwell waiting at the door like a black cloud.

"You couldn't rent a tux?" Carter asked, taking in the reporter's cheap suit jacket and blue jeans with distaste.

"No one here I need to impress," he said, those deceiving chubby cheeks stretching wide into a grin. He wondered if Jim had anyone fooled by that Jimmy Olsen mask, because all Carter saw were the beady eyes of a snake. "Thank you for the invite to this little soiree."

"No problem."

Jim looked around as if the glitter and flash of the grand ballroom was a back alley. "Hell of a way to make money for a community center. Gambling? Cash bars?"

"What the hell is your problem, Blackwell?"

Jim arched his eyebrows. "You," he said. "I thought I made that clear."

"You have questions?" Carter asked, stepping close to the man so his words didn't have to carry any further than the two of them. "Ask them. Here. Now. Stop badgering Zoe Madison."

"What are you hiding?" Jim asked. "You aren't fooling me, you know. I accuse your family of stealing gems seconds before this pregnant girl stands on a chair as a joke, and you run with the pregnant girl? It's smoke and mirrors, Carter, and I'm not buying it. I think you know where the ruby is."

"I have no idea where it is," Carter said with conviction, for the first time since the questions started to roll around. If nothing else, he could thank his mother for that.

The truth, he thought, was a revelation, so thin and slick on his tongue, unlike the years of fat, heavy lies. "And furthermore, I don't give a shit. That garbage has nothing to do with me and what I want to do for this city."

"Did your parents steal the gems in the first place?"

"I honestly don't know," he said. "I wasn't lying when I said I have no contact with them. Now call the hounds off Zoe. She has nothing to do with my family."

"But she has a lot to do with you, Carter, and that's what I'm really interested in."

"You are walking right into a harassment suit."

Jim lifted his hand and laughed, the sound as empty and flat as a dead basketball. He stepped away, knowing he was crossing a few too many lines with a lawyer. "I'll be around, Carter. I have a few more questions about this Lafayette deal."

"Lafayette is good for the city, Blackwell. What's wrong with that?"

"We'll see," Jim said, backing away, slapping his little notebook against his leg. "We'll see."

Jim walked away and Carter contemplated the advantages of the Wild West, and of being able to call an ass like Blackwell out just for being as ass.

A few people on the outskirts of the closest blackjack table glanced back at him. Or past him, actually, smiling and poking each other in the ribs. The men, particularly, seemed interested.

Carter turned and backed up, away from the gorgeous woman standing behind him on the stairs.

She wore red, scarlet really, that clung and dipped over her belly and puddled at her feet. Her arms were bare, her long elegant neck revealed. She wore diamonds at her ears and in her short black hair.

Zoe.

It was Zoe.

SHE DIDN'T EXPECT CARTER to be at the door. She'd hoped she would have a chance to circulate, get her feet under her before running into him. And then she could be casual and composed, instead of feeling like a freshman crashing the senior prom.

But no such luck. Carter was right there, stunning and big, those handsome shoulders tucked into a perfect tux.

He looked even better than she'd imagined, because he was here, in the flesh. She could reach out and touch him, feel the heat of his skin.

"Hi," she said, lifting her chin.

Head up, shoulders back, the echo of every teacher she'd ever had rang through her brain. *Feel the ceiling with the top of your head. Fill the room with your power.*

It had been awhile, but she felt the old training kick back in. Being five foot three but dancing like she was seven feet tall took a special kind of person.

She'd forgotten for a while, but she was that kind of person.

She was also apparently the kind of person who showed up at fancy fundraisers in one of Ben's drag queen dresses.

"Zoe," he breathed, clearly speechless. His eyes roved over her, warm and appreciative, leaving a giddy, sparkling heat behind.

The amazed look on his face was the best compliment she'd ever heard.

"Christ, Zoe, you're—"

A gay man's version of Marilyn Monroe, she thought.

"I'm here for me," she said instead, clumsy and loud. "For my academy."

His smile was so beautiful it nearly melted her shoulders, the steel in her spine. It wasn't just that he seemed proud, because frankly, she didn't need anyone for that. She was proud of herself. It was something far more personal. That *he* approved— this man, who was so hard on himself and so single-minded—mattered to her. Was important to her.

"Of course," he said with a short, sharp nod. "Would you like me to introduce you?"

"I would," she said, as regally as she could.

"Perhaps a quick stop by the buffet?"

She couldn't help it; she smiled, tucking her hand into his offered elbow and trying to ignore the hundred little lightning strikes between her skin and his.

"Thank you," she said as they stepped into the room, embraced by the din of a hundred people having a good time.

But she was only truly aware of him, the smooth fabric of his tux, the heat of the muscle beneath it.

"Do you...ah...play cards?" she asked as they circumvented the large puddles of people surrounding the tables.

"No," he said, all that warmth and charm suddenly gone, as if she'd imagined it all.

He took another step, but realized she wasn't moving and turned back.

"Where do you go when you do that?" she asked, ignoring the instincts that screamed at her not to care.

"Do what?" he asked, waving away a waiter with a tray of champagne.

"Get so cold like that? It's like you're here and then you're not."

He looked down at her from a great distance, despite the outrageously high—and outrageously big—heels she was wearing.

"It's an old habit," he said, his honesty surprising her. "I don't do it intentionally. I apologize."

When he looked her right in the eyes that way, revealing these strange pieces of himself, it made her nervous, as if she were naked. Or in danger.

"Apology accepted," she said, not knowing what else to say and wanting to get them back to stable, easy ground. "I, however am a great card player."

"Really?" he asked, clearly skeptical.

"Do you have to say it that way?"

"Zoe Madison, you wear every brain wave on your face, to say nothing of your emotions. You are what is called an easy mark."

"That's not true!" she gasped, and he turned to her, his eyes so hot they burned. She stepped back, surprised, but his hand at her elbow stopped her.

He half turned and she found herself in a little alcove between a curtain and a giant potted orchid. It was quiet and warm and again, the whole world shrank, everyone disappeared, leaving them alone in a giant ballroom.

"You want to be here for you," he whispered, his warm breath smelling like champagne and mint and making all the fine hair on her body rise up as if trying to pull her closer to him. "You want to believe that what you feel for me is nothing, or will go away. But underneath all your efforts to keep yourself collected and in control, what you feel for me scares you."

He was right, more than right. He'd looked straight through her and read her like a newspaper.

"I…" she stammered, her hand at her neck. Her blood pounded in her cheeks and she wished she could deny it, wished she could say anything, but she was stupid with her own horror.

"That's what I see on your face, Zoe." He leaned away from her, utterly composed. Utterly closed off, as if saying these things, seeing this warring desire inside of her were no big deal. Not to him. The unreachable Carter O'Neill.

She yanked her arm free of his fingers, ignoring the way her skin tingled.

"Do you know how embarrassing it is that you see me so clearly and I don't know a single thing about you? I can't tell if this is a game to you, or are laughing at me. I can't—"

"Look at me," he whispered.

"No!" she cried, slamming her eyes shut like a child.

"Zoe," he breathed. "Just look at me. Please."

She sighed and opened her eyes.

Magically, he'd changed. It was as if his skin had fallen off and she saw the beating heart in his chest.

He wanted her. In the same punched-in-the-stomach way she wanted him. And he was as surprised and baffled as she was by their attraction.

"We're in this together, Zoe. Whatever—" his finger touched her chest and then his, drawing a line in the air, connecting them "—this is. Despite the way it started, despite the photographers...I'm with you."

It was by far the most romantic thing anyone had ever said to her. And at this point in her life, the most unrealistic.

With me? She thought. Was that a joke? He was Carter O'Neill; he could have any nonpregnant woman in this city.

It hurt, all of it hurt. Being near this man hurt.

"Zoe?" he asked, squeezing her hand.

"Why?" she asked, the words tumbling out of her mouth. "I can't be your usual...date. I'm five months pregnant."

"I know," he said. His eyes, in the shadows, were serious and warm. Hot, actually. "Trust me," he said, laughing a little, "I know. And you're beautiful, the most beautiful woman I've ever seen."

He lifted his hands as if asking permission to touch her, and she didn't stop him. She should have, but her skin was dying for his touch, a desert without rain. His hands slid over her belly, pushing the dress over her skin, so warm and firm. "This part of you is amazing to me. You're amazing. And you're right. You're not at all like the women I usually date. But I'm so glad about that, because those women didn't have a tenth of your warmth. Or humor. Right now, I couldn't be happier, Zoe."

The baby kicked him, right in the palm, as if summoned. As if saying "nice to meet you."

"Wow," he breathed. "I can totally feel the baby."

She gasped at the pleasure of it all, his hands, her baby. It was gorgeous. The most pleasure-saturated moments of her life.

She wanted to wrap her arms around him, put her fingers in his hair and just lay one on him, right here, in front of a hundred people, as if she didn't have any control.

But she did. A little. Enough to step back and let cool air swirl between them, sweeping out the heat and smoke.

"I want to play cards," she said, her voice too loud, her whole body vibrating at the edges.

"Of course," he said indulgently.

Normally, that would make her nuts—a pampering man sounding as if he were doing a favor. But the way he said "of course," as if the only desire he had in the world was to watch her play blackjack, made her feel tingly and warm.

A woman. With a man.

They emerged from the alcove and no one

stared at them, though she was sure her blush was practically neon.

Feeling as though she were filled with ginger ale and fireflies, she turned to the closest table and found a spot at the far end, all too aware of Carter right behind her.

"Dealer wins," the dealer said. The thin blond woman swept up the cards from the last hand and stacked up the chips, tucking them into the slot built into her table. "We have a new player?" she asked, still looking down. Zoe didn't know if she was talking to her or someone else until the dealer looked right up at her. "Are you playing?"

Zoe's mouth fell open.

The dealer was the blond woman who'd paid Zoe a thousand dollars to get Carter out in that alley.

CHAPTER TEN

"WHAT ARE YOU DOING HERE?" Zoe breathed.

The woman didn't answer—she took one look at Carter and turned white, her hand holding the edge of the table as if it were keeping her upright.

Behind Zoe, where Carter stood, an arctic wind blew.

The silence was charged, electric, and Zoe didn't know much but she knew she wouldn't be playing cards here.

"No," she said quickly, but Carter interrupted.

"She'll play."

"I don't have any chips," she said as Carter nudged her into one of the chairs.

"You can buy them here," the dealer said, not making eye contact with either of them.

A hundred dollar bill floated over her shoulder and landed on the table.

"Carter—" Zoe began to rise, but Carter pushed her back into the chair.

"Buying chips," the dealer said and a woman with a tray of chips came to their table, took Carter's hundred dollar bill, and put down some blue, white and red chips.

"For charity," Carter said, his smile tight, and Zoe didn't believe it for a moment. Something terrible was going on between Carter and this woman, and Zoe wished she had a minute to talk to him, though she doubted he'd say anything at all.

Before she knew it, she had cards and a twenty-dollar bet on the table.

Zoe had a ten and a four.

"Hit," Carter said over Zoe's shoulder, and she turned to glare at him.

"I can play my own game," she said, and he nodded stiffly, his jaw so tight it looked like it could crack teeth.

The dealer flipped down another card. "Five, that's nineteen. The lady wins."

Any little surge of triumph was thwarted when Carter tossed more chips on the table over her shoulder.

"If you want to play…" she muttered.

"I don't."

Now she had an ace and a five.

"Hi—" she started to say, but again, Carter butted in.

"We're good."

Someone down the table won, and a little crowd of women cheered as Carter threw down more chips with almost violent force. The energy rolling off him was poisonous.

"I'm out," she said, standing up and stepping out of his way. Out of his gravitational pull.

"Zoe—"

"You stay and play or whatever it is you're doing, but I'm not with you on this."

She didn't stick around to hear what else he might have to say. She headed out of the ballroom toward the women's bathroom but then changed her mind and headed out a side door to a small empty courtyard surrounded by a low fence and the parking lot beyond.

She stretched her arms out, lifting her chest as if she could get more air that way, as if she could pull herself right out of this situation.

Nothing is ever just simple for me, she thought, staring up at the star-splashed sky. What rotten luck.

I like him. He likes me. And he's crazy.

Totally nuts.

Zoe wondered if the blonde was an old girl-friend. She was older, but it was hard to tell how much older.

She heard the door pop behind her and didn't even turn, sure of who it was and not knowing if she even cared enough to get involved.

"Who was that woman?" she asked.

"Well," a voice that was definitely not Carter's said, "I was sort of hoping you could tell me."

She whirled only to find Jim Blackwell, standing against the shut door and suddenly—despite the big black sky and the open night around her—she felt trapped.

"I don't know what you're talking about," she said and he only laughed.

"Leave the lying to Carter," Jim said. "He's much better at it than you."

"What do you want?" she asked, feeling slightly threatened despite his little boy looks.

"Well," he said. "I wanted to help you with your photographer problems, but you never called."

"And I won't." She thought of that horrible moment when she'd been ambushed coming out of the doctor's appointment. "The chief of police is in there," she said, pointing toward the hotel and the ballroom full of Baton Rouge and State officials. "I could talk to him about harassment."

Jim Blackwell only scoffed. "Dean Begusta wouldn't care if I stripped you naked out here."

Zoe stepped back, her heart going cold, her brain colder. Was that a threat? That was totally a threat. Wasn't it?

He stepped toward her so fast she backed up right into a wrought iron table. The clank of it was loud, but not as loud as the blood pounding in her ears. He stopped and held out his hands as if begging for a chance. "I just need to find out who that blond woman is to him—"

"I think you need to switch to a different department," Zoe said, smack-dab in the middle of something that she didn't understand. "Sports or something. Movie reviews, maybe. Because city politics is clearly making you crazy."

"No," he said, "what's making me crazy is watching O'Neill lie—"

The door behind them popped open and Zoe spun, eager for some interference. It was the blond dealer poised in the bright doorway, a cigarette in her hand.

"Sorry," she said, about to duck out.

"No!" Jim said, those little boy looks snapping back into place like a mask. *He was good,* she thought. *Good and scary.* "Come on out."

The dealer looked wary, but she stepped out anyway, the door shutting behind her, closing out the light.

Her lighter flared in the darkness, and Zoe could smell tobacco on the breeze.

The heavy air felt like trouble.

"Can I ask what your name is?" Jim asked.

"Why would you?" the dealer asked, and Zoe smiled.

Jim held out his press card. "I'm a reporter."

"Anna," she said.

"No last name?"

There was a long pause, and the tip of the cigarette burned brighter and hotter. "Nope," she said on a long exhale. Zoe honestly wished she was half as cool.

"How'd you get this job?" Jim asked.

"I'm new out at The Rouge," she said, naming one of the casinos on the river. "Owner was looking for some staff for this thing and I signed up."

"It's charity."

"So I've heard."

"You giving up your wages?"

"I don't think that's any of your damn business."

Yeah! Zoe thought, *Take that, Jim Blackwell.*

Jim didn't seem fazed. "You know Carter O'Neill?"

Zoe held her breath.

"Carter who?" Anna asked, and Jim snorted through his nose.

"You're good," he said. "But I'll find out what's going on."

He turned back to Zoe, his eyes like some kind of ooze traveling down her body, making her feel naked and gross. Like she needed a hundred showers. "May I say, you look stunning," he said.

"No," she snapped, fighting the urge to stick out her tongue. Finally he left, not back into the building, but over the small wrought iron fence and into the dark parking lot.

Zoe exhaled long and hard, her bones sagging with relief.

"You all right?" Anna asked.

"Me? Sure. I get interrogated and threatened by journalists all the time."

She took a deep breath and watched "Anna" smoke half her cigarette. "I remember you, you know. The thousand dollars."

Anna nodded.

"Is your name really Anna?" Zoe asked.

"Vanessa," she said with a small smile. "Something about that guy made me want to lie."

"How do you know Carter?" she asked, the words firing out of her mouth.

The woman looked down at her cigarette, blew ash off the glowing cherry. "You need to ask him that question," she said.

Zoe sighed. "I don't know if I want to."

"What do you mean?" the woman asked.

"Carter's like one of those pixel puzzles, you know? You stare at it and stare at it until your eyes get blurry and suddenly in all those pixels you see an ice-cream cone and then you blink and the ice-cream cone is gone. It's nothing but pixels again."

Vanessa was silent and Zoe turned to look at her.

"That doesn't make any sense," Vanessa said.

"He hides himself. He's there, and then he's not."

"Ah," Vanessa said, but that was all, and Zoe suddenly felt stupid.

"Well, lovely chatting with you, Vanessa, but I do think it's time for me to go home. This whole damn thing was a mistake."

"Zoe," Vanessa said, and Zoe paused, the door open. "Carter hasn't had it easy, you know."

Zoe blinked in surprise, but then forced herself not to care.

"Who has?" she said and stepped into the hallway.

The door shut behind her, leaving the night and the mysterious blonde outside. She glanced up and down the long hallway filled with tuxedoed men and women in gorgeous gowns and she just wanted to leave. Curl up in bed for the next four months until she had to go to the hospital.

And the next part of her life could begin.

Under her fancy red dress, her baby kicked and Zoe rubbed the spot in commiseration.

"I can't wait, either," she breathed.

"Excuse me, Zoe Madison?" a warm Southern voice drawled behind her. Zoe turned to find an older man, short and gray and built like a bulldog, but handsome in a hardworking way. Like he knew his way around a tool belt.

"Yes," she said. "Is there a problem?"

"No." The man laughed. "This is a party, so there aren't supposed to be any problems. Not for lovely women."

"Well, someone forgot to tell me that," she said with a tired smiled. "I'm heading home."

"Please," he said, touching her arm briefly when she turned to leave. "Wait. I'm Eric Lafayette. Carter O'Neill told me you're working on a program that might interest me."

Zoe's heart pounded once in her throat and her hands got clammy.

This is for me. For me and the baby and my future.

She gave herself a little pep talk and then turned on the smile. "Well, I hope I am, Mr. Lafayette, because it certainly interests me and the East Brookstown neighborhood." She smiled as bright as she could, channeling all sorts of confidence and competence.

He nodded, a bright warmth entering his black eyes. "I'm from that neighborhood," he said, and she saw stars. This was going to work. It was; she could see it right there in front of her. Her future, the future she'd come here for, was happening.

CARTER LEFT THE PARTY through the main entrance and watched Jim Blackwell storm off to his car. He knew there was a patio around here somewhere for smokers, and chances were his mother was there.

He had no idea where Zoe went.

The pool of light on the far side of the building seemed likely and he approached, stopping when he heard Zoe's voice.

Pixel puzzle.

She was right, more right than she knew. Sometimes he got so lost in his lies, his life, the constant control, that he didn't know who he was anymore.

Except when he was with Zoe. He touched her velvet skin and his body, his life, his world popped into sharp relief. He knew who he was. The things he wanted in his life seemed as if they were in the palm of his hands. She had that power. That magic.

They kept pushing each other away.

If you want her, he told himself, *you need to fight for her.*

But first he needed to find out what his mother was doing here.

He waited in the shadows of the parking lot until Zoe left, then watched his mother smoking alone at a wrought iron table and thought about Zoe. About how cold he felt and how nice it would be to warm himself by the fire that glowed in her.

"I know you're there," Vanessa said, staring down at the pack of smokes on the table.

"What are you doing here?" he asked, stepping to the edge of the light but no farther.

"I had to get a job," she said, shrugging as if it meant nothing, and he wanted to tear the world apart piece by piece. "I know the pit boss at The Rouge." Her eyes, dry and resigned, met his. "Do you want me to leave?"

She looked old. Older than he'd ever seen her. And trapped.

"What happened to all that money Margot's been giving you?" he asked.

"I owe people money." She ran her palms over her perfect hair and he watched with hate in his heart. But then, as if she just couldn't keep going, her shoulders slumped and she rested her head in her hands.

Carter stood there, unsure of what to do. When she stopped playing her part, he didn't know his.

God, there was something so alone in her. It was like all the lies and angles, the games and secrets that animated her, were turned off and she just sat there. Empty.

"Are you in danger?" he asked.

"This isn't the movies," she said. "I'm not going to get whacked." She wiped her face, her eyes, and then put her hands in her lap as if the moment were gone, the mask back on.

"So this was what…coincidence?" he asked.

"I honestly didn't know you'd be here. I wouldn't

have come if I had. I needed a job, and the only damn legal skill I have is dealing cards."

He believed her. He believed her because she looked like a woman with her back against the wall.

"It's okay. Stay," he said. "Unless you're cheating."

Her laugh was a dry empty rustle. "The pit boss would kill me."

She crushed her smoke into the ashtray.

"That reporter was giving Zoe a hard time out here," Vanessa said, and Carter's body went tight.

"He's a nuisance," Carter said.

"Is it possible she's spying on you for him?"

"No!" The thought actually made him laugh. Zoe? A spy? It was like asking a kitten to be a tiger.

"Don't be so sure," she said, watching him through ancient eyes. "She's already sold you out for a thousand dollars."

"She didn't know me," he said, and then realized that the more she knew him, and the more he treated her the way he had been, the more likely she'd sell him out for a nickel.

"Well, he's gunning for you. You got a plan?"

"It will be easier if you stay out of trouble."

Vanessa laughed. "Me? I'm just a woman

making a paycheck, Carter. Nothing wrong with that."

He felt himself smile. "Somewhere pigs are flying," he said, trying to make a joke, which was so strange. Joking with his mother—pigs really were flying.

"Well," Vanessa finally said. "You better go catch up with Zoe, before she decides you're not worth the trouble."

"I think she already has," he said, a cool wind slipping up his back.

Vanessa stood, the wrought iron chair scraping against the bricks. "Not yet," she said. "You still have a chance, trust me. That girl can't hide her emotions for shit."

He knew. It was why he liked her, why every hidden emotion he had reached out for the total honesty in her.

"Night," he said, stepping into the shadows.

"Good night, Carter," Vanessa said, her voice warm with an emotion he'd never heard before.

Inside the party, he found Zoe and Eric at a cocktail table, eating their way through what looked like a mountain of fried catfish.

"Butter-flavored Crisco," Eric was saying, his fingers greasy from the fish but his eyes warm, no doubt from a few minutes spent with Zoe.

Jealousy pulled at Carter, which was stupid, but

it was. He never got jealous, and it only proved how important she was to him. How different.

"That's the secret," Eric said.

"You're kidding!" she cried, staring down at the fish with a mix of horror and love. Carter smiled—her feelings about food were so complicated.

Eric caught sight of Carter first and he turned, graciously opening up their small circle to include him. Zoe, on the other hand, shut down, all that warmth suddenly banked at the sight of him.

No, he thought, *no no no.*

"You'll never guess, Carter," Eric said, "but we got the catfish from this soul food place on River—"

"Mama's?" Carter asked Zoe.

She nodded. "Apparently, Eric and I have similar taste." She wiped her hands off on a napkin and sighed. "Thank you, Eric. I appreciate your time and the soul food education."

"Well, I look forward to seeing you next week. Call Janet at my office and we'll get something lined up. Your academy sounds like something Baton Rouge needs."

She did it, Carter thought, sparks of pride shooting through his body. He couldn't help but grin at her, at the beauty and wonder of her. And he knew, not that it was ever in question—but he knew that Zoe was different from anyone else in his life, and not just because she was pregnant and stood on chairs and accused him of being a deadbeat daddy.

Zoe was different because he felt differently about her. He liked her and craved her. He wanted to know her better and let her know him.

He wanted to stop being a damn pixel picture.

"I will," she said, her smile bright and clean. "Thank you."

She nodded at Carter, her eyes shuttered, and he realized that he was losing his chance with Zoe before he fully knew how much he wanted it.

"Good night," Zoe said, and then she left, the sheen of her dress attracting all the light and every male eye in the room.

"That's quite a woman there, O'Neill," Eric said, his voice filled with a low-level warning. A don't-blow-this-chance alarm that Carter heard loud and clear.

"I know," he said.

He thought of his mother at that table outside, so totally alone, and he took a step after Zoe. And then another.

He didn't want to be that alone. Not anymore.

CHAPTER ELEVEN

IT WAS IMPOSSIBLE TO MAKE a graceful exit when saddled with too-big stripper shoes. Just outside the glass-and-marble lobby of the Hilton she tripped on the edge of her dress, and the shoe slipped right off her foot.

"Cinderella."

Carter came up behind her and her whole body, already electrified by the night's success, went into overload at the sight of him.

All hands on deck, her hormones screamed.

This man is too much, she tried to tell herself. *Too unpredictable. Too hot and cold. He's not right for you. For any reason.*

But he held her shoe, which looked totally ridiculous in his hand, and when she reached for it, he pulled it back.

"Let me," he said, and before she could stop him, he was crouched in front of her, brushing aside her dress, lifting her foot.

She put quivering fingertips on his shoulder.

It was the most intimate thing she'd ever felt. Ever been a part of.

His fingers on her ankles, brushing her toes, sent pulses of light and heat under her skin. As she watched, numb, all of her anger, every bit of confusion, was eradicated by the sight of him on his knee in front of her, concentrating on her ankle strap.

Without the confusion or anger, all that was left was desire. And it was a storm in her, growing out of control.

"I don't think Cinderella's shoes were this complicated," he joked, working the tiny strap at her ankle.

"They were glass slippers," she said, staring up at the stars wishing a lightning bolt would just come down and take her out of her misery. "They had their own problems."

"These don't even fit you."

"They belong to a gay drag queen," she blurted.

"Oh," he said, and she slapped her head, glad he wasn't looking at her. His finger trailed up her instep as he stood, leaving fireflies dancing along her spine, the nape of her neck. "That explains it then."

His smile was so sweet. Tender. As if the scene in the ballroom with the dealer had never happened. Suddenly she couldn't stand it, the way her body stayed warm for this man, no matter what he did.

He was close, so close that she could lean against him and all that heat would be hers. All that electricity would blast through her, obliterating her better sense, her concerns and doubts.

She could just feel. For the first time in a year, she could lean back into a man's arms and just feel.

The temptation was intense, like standing in front of a blast furnace in a fur coat.

But she took a step away, refusing to follow his lure like some dumb fish, attracted to shiny objects. She was better than that.

"Who is she?" she asked. "The dealer."

Carter's face turned to stone, and she knew that if he didn't answer her, she'd leave and never think of him again. Never want him. Never dream of his hands and those lips—ever again.

This ill-conceived affair would be over before it really began.

"My mother," he breathed.

Shock rippled through her. Over her and around her. It was hard, actually, not to laugh in sheer nervous reaction.

"Your mo—" Carter put his finger against her lips, a touch that gathered and pulled between her legs, nearly knocking her to her knees.

"Please," he whispered, looking somehow pained and lost, as if saying the word *mother* had ripped the skin off an old wound. "Not here. I'll tell you, just not here. I'm sorry for the way I acted in there. It was a shock…I guess…to see her. I reacted badly."

Zoe ran a trembling hand over her hair.

It was one thing to desire him. Another to like him. But this…this new river of sneaky, dangerous emotion that began to swirl through her needed to be avoided. She would not care. No. She couldn't. Caring would be a disaster.

"I'll take you home," he said, apparently reading her sudden misgivings.

He lifted his finger to summon a cab as if the usually elusive creature were simply a dog waiting for a command.

Quickly, she reached up and pulled down his arm. She wouldn't care about him, but she didn't want to go home. Her home was sad. Empty.

His eyes flared as if thinking what she was thinking. That this night, despite its wild ups and downs of surprise and success, was too lonely.

"You want to go celebrate?" he asked. "The beginning of your academy? We could go get some pie."

"I'm not hungry," she said.

"I think hell just got chilly."

She smirked and shook out her hands, flooded with nervous energy. The excitement of the night, being with this man, made her feel a little too alive in her skin. As if she'd had too much coffee. "I would walk, though."

"In those shoes?"

"I've got sneakers in my car," she said, leading him toward her station wagon up the street.

A walk was safe. She wouldn't have to worry about cozy alcoves or him touching her feet. She could cool down, get her hormones back under control.

But he tucked her hand into his arm and the tension of his muscles under the fine fabric of his jacket felt anything but safe.

"AMELIA?" HE ASKED AN HOUR later as they walked along the river. "Are you giving birth to an old woman?"

"What's wrong with Amelia?"

"Nothing. If you're eighty years old."

"It's a lovely name," she said, feeling as if the night had taken a magical turn and had suddenly been dipped in sugar. Within the first ten minutes of their walk down Third Street, she'd given up any notion of feeling safe with this man. They walked side by side, his hip rubbing hers, his muscles under her hands, and now she was charged with power.

A humming desire churned through her, and every time he turned, putting his hand to the small of her back, she felt like she could light up the night.

"You know for sure you're having a girl?"

"The doctors haven't told me, but I know."

"Feminine intuition?"

"Don't laugh."

"I'm not. I have great respect for feminine intuition." His grin was boyish, and she was so intrigued, so beguiled it was hard not to curl herself into his arms and push back the wind-tousled hair over his forehead.

"I just feel like I know this little person and I know she's a girl. Like I understand her and she understands me and we're making our way through this together."

She honestly didn't understand why she was talking to him like this, as if these little secrets, these details about the way her brain worked, were nothing. Small talk. Flirtation even. She kept laying herself out there like it didn't matter.

His fingers feathered through her hair, brushing it off her face, and she nearly sighed with pleasure. But then his fingers were gone and she awkwardly turned away, staring at the city decked out in its Christmas finery.

White lights on the trees, the old state building lit up in red and green.

"It's pretty, isn't it?" he said.

"It is," she agreed, surprised he thought so. "You like Christmas?"

He shrugged. "I did, you know, as a kid. I suppose now it's just another day."

"My mother goes overboard," Zoe said. "Starts shoving Christmas down my throat right after Halloween. I've started to like Easter just to be contrary."

His lip kicked up, but his eyes were still on the city. "I envy you," he said. "With the baby. You have a reason to love the holidays again. So many traditions to pass on. When I was a kid, my grandmother used to make us wait on the stairs until she'd showered and done her hair and put on her makeup." He smiled, shaking his head. "It was torture. I can't wait to do that to my kids."

She laughed, her heart pounding as she imagined a bunch of little blond kids groaning on the stairs while some lucky woman watched Carter shave very slowly.

"That's a good tradition," she whispered and turned, staring down at the river, the wind cooling her cheeks.

"It looks clean, doesn't it?" she asked, looking down at the churning black waters below them.

"It's dark," he said. "Clean, dirty, everything looks the same in the dark."

"That's a pretty pessimistic view from a politician."

Carter laughed, turning his back to the water to face the buildings behind them. The Christmas lights of the city reflected in his eyes. "Maybe it is," he said, his voice dark with something she couldn't quite place.

"Have you always wanted to be a politician?"

"No." He laughed. "I wanted to be a skateboarder, remember?"

"Of course, such a natural progression from skater boy to mayor."

Carter was quiet for a long time, and Zoe found a huge wealth of patience inside of her for this man. She would wait for him to talk, no matter how long it took.

"My family is…unorthodox."

"Your mother?"

"The tip of the iceberg, sadly. My mother has spent most of her life as a petty crook. She did some time a dozen years ago, but for the most part has managed to be good enough to stay out of trouble, but not good enough to ever be able to leave the game. She left us on my grandmother's doorstep when we were kids and Margot raised us."

"Your grandmother? That doesn't sound too illicit."

Carter laughed. "In her heyday, Margot was the paid companion of mobsters and musicians and politicians. She taught us how to play poker and handicap horse races. By the time I was fifteen, I could cheat at cards and hold my gin better than a man twice my age."

She wasn't sure that laughter was the right reaction to this news, so she bit her tongue.

Carter glanced over at her, his face tight. "I've never told anyone this."

A warm sun rose inside of her, a sense of pride that she was the one to receive this kind of trust. This kind of intimacy. "You're ashamed?" she asked.

He pursed his lips as if weighing his answer. "Yeah, I guess. In a way. I think going into law and politics was my way of rebelling. As ridiculous as that sounds."

"It doesn't sound ridiculous at all."

"My brother is, or was actually, a big deal poker player, before he married a cop. My sister married the son of a gem thief who used to work with my father—"

"And you want to do good."

"Right, it does sound ridiculous."

"It doesn't," she breathed. He didn't look at her and she could see his discomfort, the tension in his muscles.

"I don't actually know if I would be a good mayor," he said.

"What do you mean?" she asked, stunned to see such doubt in him.

He glanced at her askance. "Come on, you saw me at Jimmie Simpson. Those women hated me and I couldn't…" He sighed. "I couldn't win them over."

She licked her lips, wondering if she was about to overstep some boundary, but he'd made fun of her baby's name, so fair was fair.

"First of all," she said. "Those women are tough and no one has an easy time winning them over. I've gone up against Tootie Vogler in the past and she made mincemeat out of me."

He turned to face her fully, a smile playing about his lips. "But?"

"But you were being patronizing," she said, and winced, waiting for him to snap.

He simply stared at her.

"You mad?"

"No," he said. "I think you're right. I think…" His eyes roved over her face and she was suddenly spellbound. Breathless. "You're amazing," he whispered.

She cupped his face in her hands, his skin warm against her flesh, the beginning of a beard rough in her palms. She wished she could hold all of him this way, every wounded and taut inch of him.

She turned his head so he had no choice but to meet her eyes.

"I think, despite your family, you're a good man."

"If you knew—" He shook his head.

"If I knew what?"

He stared into her eyes and she couldn't breathe. Her heart hammered in her chest. His fingers touched her cheek, the glittery barrette in her hair. "I think maybe I've said enough tonight," he said. "What is it about you, Zoe? You make a mess of me."

As compliments went, it was a pretty mixed message, but she understood what he was saying and her heart swelled.

"It's late," he whispered.

"It is," she agreed, not moving. She couldn't have, not for the life of her. He'd said they were in this together, and the look in his eyes when he'd said it had made her believe him.

It might be a mistake, but she wasn't going home. Not alone. Not after this night.

Her weight shifted onto her toes and she tilted, swayed right against his chest.

"Take me to your house," she whispered, hoping that was all she would have to say.

He groaned as the fireworks exploded between their bodies. Her skin transmitted the slick cool feel of his tux to the rest of her body.

"You sure, Zoe? I don't want to rush—"

"I do," she said. "I really want to rush into this."

They turned, his arm a mantle around her

shoulders as they stepped to the curb where he got a cab in record time.

He was a magician, she thought, and couldn't wait until he got those magic hands on her.

After opening the door, he bent to her and helped her into the backseat. She felt every inch of his body against hers and the hormones, the crazed craving hormones, roared to life and every cell in her being wanted Carter.

Craved Carter.

"Perkins Road," he said to the cabbie.

The door slammed shut behind him and the car took off into the night.

Holy Crap, Zoe thought. *I'm really doing this. I am going to have sex with Carter.*

"I had no idea you lived there," she babbled, nerves making a fool of her. She was going to get naked in front of a lover for the first time in a very, very long time and she no longer had her dancer's body. "Is that a house? Or a condo? I've seen the condos around there. Very nice—"

His fingertips brushed her cheek, and she lost all her breath, just deflated against the cracked plastic seat beneath her.

"You're beautiful when you're nervous," he whispered, his words like sparks against her skin.

Their eyes caught and held and the fire between them exploded into flames.

His thumb pressed down on her lower lip,

touching her tongue, and she licked his thumb into her mouth.

"Zoe," he whispered, his fingers cradling her cheek, and the heat between her legs grew damp.

His blue eyes blazed and the air radiated between them. She bit the pad of his thumb, licked it in apology, and his lips parted and drew a ragged breath.

Power, she thought. *I have such power.* It had been a long time since she'd been drunk, but this was so much better than that.

In this together, he'd said, and she didn't doubt it. Right now, the whole world could go up in flames and they wouldn't notice. Wouldn't care.

All that mattered was this man's touch, his fingers and the pulse of her flesh, the appetite of her sex.

"Ah…we're here?" the cabbie said and Zoe jerked away, but Carter gripped her hand, keeping her present and with him. The world didn't matter, his touch said. They can think what they want. He tossed the cabbie a couple of bills and pulled her out of the cab.

They stepped out onto the curb, and she barely had a chance to take in the handsome condo complex, one of the new developments on Perkins Road. All windows and brick. No plants or flowers. Not a curtain in a window.

So like him. Unreadable, sort of. Closed off. Handsome, but cold.

Don't care, she reminded herself. *Don't start counting all the ways this man could hurt you.*

"Zoe?" he said, "are you—"

She kissed him, throwing herself against the strength of his body. Her hands wove into his hair and gripped it in her fists.

He moaned and pulled her as close as he could, as if he were trying to tuck her into his skin. His arms, so wide and big, felt like bands across her back. And his lips. His lips were delicious. Salty and sweet. Better than salsa and ginger cookies. Better even, than Frayley's beignets.

His hands gripped the silk of the dress, and as his lips parted the kiss started to spin someplace dark. Exciting.

His tongue licked her, his lips sucked at her and the heat that had cooled with her doubts exploded inside her all over again, sharp and painful. A brutal awareness of her skin, of every pleasure center, clamored to be dealt with.

She wanted to do filthy things with this man. Gorge herself on sex and Carter.

"Hey," she whispered. "I…um…can you?"

"Can I what?"

"It's the hormones," she said, like it was a warning.

"You want to roll me in caramel sauce?"

Oh, that sounded good. That sounded so good.

"Just spill it, Zoe."

"Can you be...kinky?"

His smile split open the night. "Try me," he whispered, and swung her into his arms.

CHAPTER TWELVE

CARTER WAS NERVOUS. Like a virgin. He wished he could blame it on the pregnancy, but he knew, deep down, he was nervous because this was Zoe. Zoe in his arms, Zoe in his bed. In his house.

He hadn't done this in a long time, brought a woman home. It had grown too personal and he couldn't concentrate wondering what they were seeing when they looked at his things.

But not Zoe. Zoe had already seen so much of him. What would looking at some art, or his dirty kitchen, possibly change?

He set Zoe down and unlocked the door, pushed it open and then closed it behind them. It was dark in his house, warm, and it felt like the night was a part of them. He could feel her in the air, as if she were electricity.

And maybe she was.

Kinky.

Was she kidding? Could she be any more beautiful? More exciting?

Zoe stepped into a bright square of light that fell in from the bank of windows in his living room.

Her skin glowed pale and perfect, as if she were made of moonlight.

She smiled, shy, but knowing her beauty. Christ. He wanted to eat her. He wanted to lay her down on the floor and spread her out.

Kinky, he thought, a devilish thrill making him feel ten feet tall swirling through him. Where to start?

"Take off your dress," he said.

"Here?"

He nodded.

Something about the command in his voice killed the hesitancy in her face. Now she was all woman.

Her hands found the zipper under her arm and pulled it down, inch by tantalizing inch.

She was Marilyn Monroe. Hell, she was Eve. She was everything beguiling and gorgeous and feminine.

The dress dipped at her chest and she clasped it to her, hiding her naked body from his eyes and making him want to roar and pull it off her.

"Take off your coat," she whispered, licking her lips.

Every ounce of blood in his body pooled in his crotch and he could barely think.

Mindless, he ripped off his jacket and tore open his shirt, sending buttons flying into the shadows. He heard one hit his TV.

He stepped toward her and she retreated. She gave him a smile, a flash of flesh, and adrenaline spiked his blood.

"Your dress, Zoe," he nearly growled.

She shook her head, stepping backward into the dark and then into another square of light. She kicked off her shoes and he toed off his. Again, she stepped backward out of the light, her eyes glowing in the dark. He took a deep breath and stepped into the light she'd left, and he knew she could see every line of his body. Every thought and emotion on his face. He was more than naked. Worse than naked.

He was revealed.

And totally turned on.

He lowered his hands to his belt, opened the leather and metal clasp.

"Is this what you want?" he asked. "A show?"

He could feel her desire pulsing through the air. Her hand, white and elegant, reached out of the darkness and touched his fly, the hard ridge of his erection beneath the fabric. Her fingers stroked him; her palm flattened and pressed hard against him. "This is what I want," she whispered.

He tilted his head back and dropped his hands, surrendering to everything—the moment, Zoe.

Yes, he thought, *yes, please yes. Touch me.*

Her warm hands made quick work of the zipper, and he felt his pants bag at the waist, fall to his knees, and he kicked out of them. He glanced down at her hands, easing into the band of his underwear and then…*oh*.

"Zoe," he groaned, grabbing her wrist, probably too hard, but he didn't care. Couldn't stop himself. Her fingers toyed with the thick head of his penis, feathered down the shaft.

He was going to die. Right now.

He pulled on her wrist, bringing her into the light where she stood, gasping. And naked.

Her breasts were pink and perfect, the nipples hard in the bright light. Her skin stretched like ivory velvet over sleek muscles, but the best part was the thin wisp of lace he could barely see because of the gorgeous mound of her belly.

"Look at you," he breathed, and she pulled her hands free to put them on her belly.

"I know," she whispered, her voice broken and soft. "It's strange, right? This is—"

"You're gorgeous," he said. Not even realizing what he was doing he dropped to his knees, face to navel with her belly. He kissed her skin, stroked the contours of her stomach. Maybe it would be strange to other men, but he found her impossibly sexy. The most womanly thing he'd ever been privileged to touch.

"Oh." She sighed. "Oh, wow."

He could smell her desire and he smiled wickedly against her skin. Sliding his hands up her legs, he found the edges of the thong, the lace damp under his fingers. She jolted. Twitched.

Her fingers slid into his hair, pulling a little, and the violence fed his desire. He pressed his face to the thin lace, felt the curls against his lips. His fingers teased their way inside the lace and she began to shake, to quiver and moan, and Carter smiled with sudden secret knowledge.

Zoe Madison was hot. She was wet. And she was going to fall apart in his arms like no other woman he'd ever known.

Rough now, because he was losing all control, he pulled the lace from her body and his lips found the hard edge of her clitoris, his fingers the deep damp well of her womanhood, and within moments he brought Zoe to her knees.

"MORE," SHE WHISPERED, once she could speak again. She was straddling his lap, the hard press of his erection against her belly. It was as if the orgasm had only increased her appetite, and now she shook for the man.

She kissed his damp lips, tasted herself on him and felt the fires burn hotter. "I want more," she breathed against his lips, her fingers gripping his erection. She licked her thumb, her eyes locked on his, and circled the head of his penis.

She loved his control right now, the edge of his jaw, the burn of his eyes. Oh, that control was really the sexiest thing about him, because she knew what was on the other side of it.

A man unleashed.

And she really, really wanted him unleashed. That would be great; it would be totally fantastic. She just had to get him there.

His fingers slid back between her legs. "I'll give you more," he breathed. "I'll give you as much as you can take."

She wiggled away from his hands, sliding off his legs.

He was gorgeous in this light. All hard smooth muscles. She licked his nipple and he groaned, his fingers fisting in her hair.

Oh, she thought, *I like that.* To get more of it, she sucked on his nipple, bit gently with her teeth until he swore and arched against her.

Yes, she thought.

A man unleashed. We're getting there.

She leaned back and looked up into his shuttered, smoldering eyes. He was still trying so hard to keep his control, but she was just going to have to try harder to break it.

Resting her weight on one arm behind her, she spread her legs, and his eyes blazed, drawn like a magnet to the damp curls he'd explored oh so thoroughly.

What to do? she thought, delighted and burning, feverish with this need to pull him apart. She touched her own breast, squeezing the nipple, and he groaned, his hands in fists at his side.

"Get up on your knees," she whispered.

He quirked his eyebrow, but didn't do it.

"Please," she whispered. He smiled but still didn't do it, watching her hand as her fingers toyed with her nipple.

Devil, she thought, her breath caught in her throat. Slowly, his eyes watching her every move, she put her hand between her legs, her thumb brushed her clitoris and she felt the surge of another orgasm coming.

"You feel so good," he said. "Don't you?"

She stopped, her body beginning to shake. This was supposed to break *his* control—hers was already broken.

"Up on your knees," she said, and he shifted, every muscle flexing and moving, like a statue brought to life.

His erection pulsed in her hands and she kissed the head, felt it leap against her lips.

"Zoe," he moaned, his voice broken and hot as if burned by a terrible fire. She licked him, sucked him. Did every wicked thing to him that he'd done to her.

"Touch yourself," he breathed. "Touch yourself while you suck me."

Oh! she thought. *So dirty!* It was sinful, depraved, but she did it, her fingers in her damp curls, her secret places.

His fingers, so big and callused, touched her hand, driving her faster against herself until a giant wave lifted her up.

"No," she said, pushing his hands away.

"I thought you wanted more," he said, the devil in his eyes. His lips.

"With you," she whispered, looking him in the eye as she licked him, top to bottom. He shook, small tremors really that she could only feel because she was right there, pressed against him. Her mouth was full of him, her body ached for him and her heart…well, her heart needed to mind its own business. Her body was running this show.

"I'm not—" His smile was broken. Chagrined. His fingers touched her neck, lifted her chin until he slipped away from her. "I'm going to lose it, Zoe," he said as if it were a bad thing.

"That's sort of the idea," she said, getting to her knees, so close to him her breasts dragged up against his chest. Again she felt his shaking.

"I…" His hands touched her stomach, cupped her breasts. His thumbs stroked her nipples. "I don't want to hurt you," he said, laying a hand flat against the swell of her belly. It was so tender, the most tender touch she'd ever felt in her life, and her heart strained hard against her chest, a bird beating at its cage.

"You won't hurt me," she said, trying to muscle her heart out of the picture, because she was beginning to feel less like a porn star and more like a woman in danger of falling in love.

And really, she was going for porn star here.

"You make me a little crazy," he said, kissing her lips, breathing across her neck until her nipple was in his mouth and it felt like she was being licked by fire.

"Okay," she sighed, her mind going blank, every word she knew running away from her. "That's… great. I…ah…oh wow…want you crazy."

He bit her, just hard enough to light up every single jackpot sign in her body.

"Good," he said, his voice all dark again, like chocolate and velvet and she felt that wave building in her. Was she going to come just listening to him talk? She squeezed her thighs together. "Because I want you in my bed."

She whimpered as he scooped her up, her legs around his waist, the head of his erection bumping the white-hot center of her body. He walked through the shadows, the darkness a living breathing heat around them. She felt like they were cocooned, safe.

Her back pressed open a door and then she was bounced onto a soft mattress, a silky comforter against her skin.

Carter opened the drawer by his bed and pulled

out a condom. She turned her head to watch him unwrap it and roll it over his penis. Sexy, she thought, and she'd never thought that before.

Everything this man did was sexy. She could watch him file taxes and be turned on.

His hands slipped up her legs and suddenly yanked her, pulling her hips off the edge of the tall mattress. His smile was wicked, delicious, his touch sure and confident. Her legs twined around his hips, her weight balanced in his hands. Despite her belly, the pregnancy, she felt so small against him. She arched her back, notching herself against him.

Sweat pooled between them, their panting and the rustle of her body against the comforter the only sounds in the room.

Still he waited, pulling the moment so taut she thought she might snap.

"Cart-ah!" she cried as he entered her, driving so deep she felt him in the back of her throat. Her body clenched him in hard triumph. So long, she thought. Oh, it had been so long.

"Are you okay?" he asked, leaning over her, his face etched with concern.

She laughed—she couldn't help it. Running her hands over his shoulders, cupping the muscles, testing her fingernails against his skin—she laughed, delighted in the feel of him.

Rocking hard against him, she arched her back, feeling every inch of him, every inch of her body.

"Oh," she sighed. "I'm so good."

He leaned over her, his hair falling over his eyes, and she reached up to touch his face. She arched again and watched his control begin to fray moment by moment, touch by touch.

Yes, she thought, glee riding her heartbeat. *Yes!*

Carter was gorgeous this way, human and vulnerable. She knew, in a wild tender moment, that this was a gift. Carter, with no defenses, his heart in his eyes, was a rare gift.

He drove her back on the mattress, shuddering against her. She held him as hard as she could in her arms, while trying to keep him far away from her heart.

ZOE KNEW MISTAKES. She was an idiot savant with mistakes. If there was some kind of game show—Name That Mistake—she'd be a millionaire. A grand champion.

And as she watched the sun rise outside his window, turning the sky pink and pale yellow, tracing early-morning clouds in white-hot light, she knew that making love to Carter had been a doozy of a mistake.

Her baby slept under her hand, and Carter slept beside her, facedown in a pile of pillows. She forced herself not to look at him, not to push the hair out of his face so she could see his lips. Count his eyelashes.

She closed her burning eyes and swore under her breath.

Last night had opened up some hidden chamber of want, of craving. And it was all focused on Carter.

Her mother's voice rang in her head—"You're a single mother and this is no time to fall in love."

Once again, her mom was right. Right man. Wrong time.

So, it was time for this particular mistake to end.

Quietly, carefully, she slipped out from under the silky gray comforter and tried as hard as she could not to notice other details of his bedroom. Like the painting over his bed; moonlight on water, a lonely boat in the foreground.

She could tell herself to stop caring, but it was too late. Because when she saw that painting she thought of Carter, so alone. Everywhere she looked, she saw parts of Carter that made him more endearing to her.

Last night, when Carter's control had snapped, something had snapped in her, too, and she needed to get away from him, get back to her home, her pig mugs and yoga pants. Real life.

Every Cinderella night had an expiry date, and she'd hit hers.

The white-faced alarm clock on the dresser said that it was 7 a.m., and if she didn't go now, he'd be awake and they'd make love again. Or worse, they'd talk, and he'd already pushed her to all her crumbling, unsafe edges.

In the living room, her dress was a scarlet puddle in the middle of the shiny mahogany floors and she shimmied into it, looking for her underwear. Under her bare feet it felt as though the wood carried the remnants of the heat between them, as if scorch marks might mar the surface.

The need to leave became urgent. She felt shaky, barely in control. She'd leave her underwear; the glitter of a barrette under the couch barely distracted her.

She scooped up her shoes and purse, and after a moment's consideration, she grabbed Carter's dress shirt and threw it on over her dress.

She felt so naked, so ridiculous in an evening gown on a Sunday morning.

Her hand just touched the solid brass knob when a knock thundered against the door.

"Uncle Carter!" A girl's voice screamed from the hallway.

Uncle Carter? Zoe mouthed, dread a hundred-pound weight in her stomach.

"Open up!" The girl's voice accompanied another barrage of knocks.

This is bad, Zoe thought, backing away from the door until she ran into something warm. Hard.

Carter.

CHAPTER THIRTEEN

"CRAP," SHE WHISPERED and winced, unable to turn around. He had to know what she was doing, sneaking out with the dawn. Like a coward.

Or worse.

"Are you okay?" his dark voice rumbled. His breath rustled her hair and her skin nearly purred.

She nodded, her throat closed tight against the thousand things she wanted to say.

He was quiet, his chest rising and falling behind her, and finally she worked up the nerve to face him. It was Carter all right, but changed somehow. That control that had crumbled last night was back in place, but slightly different. Weak in places.

And she could see all too clearly, that her attempt at sneaking off hurt him.

"I'm sorry, Carter," she breathed in a quick rush. "I…just need to go home. This…last night…"

"Of course," he agreed, without really agreeing. Such a politician, she thought.

He picked up his underwear and pants from the floor and tugged them on, each motion succinct and restrained. He didn't say a word but she could feel the disappointment rolling off him.

"I can't care about you, Carter," she whispered, and his motions stilled for the barest moment, a hesitation so quick she would have missed it if she hadn't been staring at him so hard.

She willed him to understand how fragile her heart was, how complicated her life would become.

"Carter!" the little girl yelled again. "Open the door!"

"My niece," he said with a smile that nearly broke her heart. "I'd tell you to leave out the back door, but I don't have one." He put his hand to the door. "You'll just have to tough this out."

"Carter!" she squealed. "Don't—"

But then the door was open and a nine-year-old girl, a cyclone, her long red hair in stiff braids down her back, was hurling herself against Carter's legs, and he was laughing, stroking her head and trying to keep his balance.

He picked her up, gave her a funny shake.

It was Carter as she'd never seen him. Never guessed he could be.

Her baby kicked, hard, and Zoe took it as a warning. If she stayed, she'd be in trouble—her little boat, barely afloat on the sea of things she could feel for this man, would capsize and she'd drown in unwanted emotion.

She turned, ready to make her escape before having to explain what she was doing in Uncle Carter's house, in his shirt and no underwear.

And she nearly ran right into a blond woman who looked so much like Carter and so much like the woman he'd said was his mother that she could only be one person.

"Hi!" the woman said, her twinkling, knowing eyes missing no detail about Zoe's barely zipped dress and Carter's bare chest. "I'm Savannah," she said, holding out her hand. "That's my daughter, Katie."

"Zoe," Zoe managed to stammer past the huge boulder of embarrassment lodged in her throat. Savannah wore a clingy blue top that revealed the very small swell of a pregnant belly. Or too big a lunch, it was hard to say. "Madison."

"Are you a friend of Uncle Carter's?" The red-headed cyclone asked, wedged against Carter's side. "Because we brought Thanksgiving." She looked up at her uncle with hero worship pouring from her eyes. "Mom said you'd never remember that Thanksgiving's on Thursday so we needed to bring you some food so you wouldn't starve because all the restaurants will be closed and you're far too important to come home for the holiday."

"She said all that, did she?" Carter grumbled.

"Please, stay," Savannah said to Zoe. "We've got plenty of food."

"Zoe was leaving," Carter said, his voice so cold it blew frost across her skin, but Savannah shot him an acidic look.

The baby kicked again, a wicked one-two combination, and Zoe put her hand under her belly in comfort.

A move Savannah did not miss and Zoe knew that under the white dress shirt, Savannah saw that she was pregnant. Her eyes went wide and her mouth dropped open.

"You," she breathed to Carter, "have some explaining to do." Savannah looked like an angry teacher about to give one hell of a lecture that Zoe wanted no part of.

"The baby isn't his," Zoe said.

Savannah's eyes narrowed even farther. "Is it your husband's?"

Zoe stared dumbstruck and Carter laughed. "She's not married, Savannah. You can retract the fangs. And there's no need for you to pretend to be a prude. Zoe's an adult. I'm an adult. And she was leaving."

"You don't have to say it like that," Zoe grumbled, glaring at him.

"Am I wrong?" he asked, one of those fine eyebrows arching, making him look like some unforgiving ruler. "You weren't sneaking out of here without saying goodbye?"

Mortified to be having this conversation in front

of a kid and Carter's sister, Zoe glanced sideways at Savannah, who held up her hands. "We'll be in the kitchen. And for what it's worth—I hope you stay." She laughed and shook her head before picking up two big totes that wafted delicious smells and hustling her daughter through a far doorway. "I mean I really hope you stay," she yelled over her shoulder.

And then they were gone and it was only Carter watching her, unreadable as ever. Bright sunlight flooded the room and illuminated every dark corner, making it impossible for her to ignore all those things she didn't want to see. The pieces of him on display. Photographs on the wall of a trio of blond kids and an older woman around a giant cypress. Books in a book shelf—the man liked Mark Twain.

The running shoes, slumped by the door, an iPod tucked into them.

She wanted to close her eyes and clamp her hands over her ears, but she couldn't. She'd gotten herself here and now it was time to get herself out.

"I'm going to have a baby," she whispered.

Carter's lips curled. "I know."

She took a deep breath and put it all on the line. "It's one thing to have a one-night stand—I can handle that. But if we keep going like this—dates and sex and meeting your family—it's going to hurt when you leave."

"Who said I was leaving?" he asked, crossing his arms over his chest. "Maybe you'll leave. You already seem halfway out the door."

"Don't be obtuse."

"Then don't be a coward."

She glared at him, and he ran his hands through his hair, putting it all on end. It was adorable.

She glared harder.

Her mother's words came back to her, all her warnings about being a single mother, about the perils of following one's heart instead of one's head.

Only pain, her mother always said, is guaranteed.

"Look, Zoe," he breathed, dropping his arms to his side and looking somehow deflated. "Last night…I didn't bring you here and make love to you lightly. I knew what I was doing. Now my sister's here and she's brought food, and I'll bet it's sugar pie—which you will love. You can stay, see what happens, or you can go." He shrugged as if all of this was no big deal, and it made her feel totally unreasonable. Foolish, for thinking they were walking into a disaster. But they had to be. Honestly, how else could this end?

She was a pregnant dance teacher without insurance, and he was probably going to be mayor by the end of next year.

"I would like you to stay," he said, leaving her speechless and weak. All those reasons why making love to him was a mistake, why staying here with him was a catastrophe—were so far away. She couldn't remember them so well anymore.

Carter turned, walking across the room toward the bright kitchen with the yummy smells and the sound of a kid laughing. Here in his house. She never expected it, would never have guessed this kind of scene could take place in this house. It was like finding caramel under rock—a sweet surprise where she never dreamed it would be.

And if she left, what else would she miss?

Besides sugar pie, which frankly sounded worth staying for.

But this man, this beautiful man with the filthy mind and the broken control and the niece like a firecracker—what other secrets would he show her, if she stayed? If she had the courage to stay?

Stay or go? she thought.

Head or heart?

She rubbed her fingers over the taut lines of her belly, felt the kick and flutter of the baby under her fingers.

She did not want to put her baby in the strange prison Zoe's mother had put her in.

Just the two of them. Forever.

And maybe there was no guarantee with Carter, but when had she ever needed one? She'd gone into dance knowing that one misstep, one injury, might end her career. There was never a guarantee with any man she ever dated—did she think there was going to be one now? Was she never going to date again, unless the man had some kind of feelings-back guarantee?

Her decision to be a single mom had been the riskiest thing she'd ever taken on and she'd done that knowing what she was getting into.

There were no guarantees. In life. Love. She knew that. It was what she liked about life. What she loved about it.

Zoe's stomach growled and the baby kicked and the decision was made.

She followed him into the kitchen.

CARTER WAS HAVING an out-of-body experience; it was the only explanation. His pregnant sister and his pregnant…Zoe were talking about Bonne Terre, his family home, like it was Tara before the war.

"It sounds beautiful," Zoe whispered, her eyes alight. Of course she would love Bonne Terre, the mystery and romance of it. What he remembered of it was being left there by a mother who didn't love him enough to stay.

"It's falling down," Carter said. "She's not telling you that part."

"No, Carter, if you ever came home you'd know we're fixing it up. It's beautiful now. Again."

He glanced sideways at Katie while he and his niece unloaded mountains of Thanksgiving Day food. Turkey and stuffing, cranberry sauce. Two sugar pies.

"It's nice," Katie said, nodding enthusiastically. "After Matt fell through the floor in the foyer, they fixed up everything."

He heard Zoe laugh behind him and his whole body smiled.

"Did you already have Thanksgiving?" he asked Katie, wondering where all this food had come from.

"Mom's practicing," Katie said. "Matt's dad, Joel, is coming and she wants everything to be perfect. Also, Mom likes eating piles of stuffing."

"She eating a lot?" Carter asked, watching his sister and Zoe out of the corner of his eye. How was this moment even possible? It was odd enough having his sister here, but Savannah and Zoe sat there as if they'd known each other their whole lives.

Maybe it was a woman thing.

Or maybe it was the magic of Zoe.

"Tyler says she's eating for four," Katie whispered, "but he only says that when she's not around."

"Ty's no dummy," Carter said, and was suddenly overwhelmed by how much he missed his family. The longing to see his brother was so sharp he braced himself against the counter. Ty, who made life seem so easy, who practically glittered when he walked.

The last time they'd all been together, Ty had told Carter to stop protecting them from their mother, that they were adults and he could cut the protective big brother act.

Ty had said it like it should be easy. Like Carter's whole life wasn't sewn up in the act.

"Carter?" Zoe asked from across the room, and he blinked back the ridiculous tears. "You okay?" she asked, and he wondered how she knew—what sixth sense she had about him that warned her when he was running low on control.

Savannah watched it all with hope written all over her face. Hope that he would fall in love, not be so lonely—it was written in big block letters right across her forehead.

Suddenly he wasn't sure if having Zoe here was a good idea. It was one thing to have her in his life here, in Baton Rouge, but it was another thing to involve her with his family. He kept those parts of his life separate for so long and she wouldn't understand that. Zoe would blur the lines and make a mess of the rules he lived by.

"Carter?" It was Savannah this time, her voice sharp, and he realized he was being rude.

"Sorry. I'm hungry. How about you?"

She nodded, her smile cautious but happy, and he started making plates for all of them, happy to have something to do.

"Uncle Carter?" Katie whispered.

"What?" he whispered back, loading a plate into the microwave.

"Is she your girlfriend?"

Carter glanced back at his niece and her bright eyes and then past her to where Zoe sat at the table.

Last night had been amazing—there was no doubt about it. But they were both still surrounded by hard shells of secrets.

"I don't know," he said. For now. But when he told her the truth about lying in court, would she still want to be with him? And when, and if, she told him about the father of the baby—maybe there was something in that story that would change the way he felt about her. Though he couldn't imagine what that could be.

"Have you asked her?" Katie asked.

"You think I should?" he asked.

Katie shrugged, the nine-year-old sage. "It's a big move, Uncle Carter. A big move."

You don't know the half of it, he thought. He picked his niece up and gave her a squeeze before throwing her over his shoulder and walking with her and two full plates of food over to the table.

"So?" Savannah asked, picking at a piece of turkey. "How did you two meet?"

Carter opened his mouth, a vague lie at his lips.

"Your mother, actually," Zoe said, digging into a pile of mashed potatoes.

Savannah's gaze was a knifepoint against his throat.

"Do tell," she said through her teeth.

"VANESSA HAS A *job*?" Savannah asked after Carter had filled his sister in on their mother's latest foray into their lives. Katie had been sent into the living room to watch TV and the plates of Thanksgiving Day food were growing cold in front of them. Even Zoe wasn't eating. "She's what, living here? In Baton Rouge?"

Savannah looked dejected, her shoulders slightly slumped, the light in her eyes diminished. As if just hearing about Vanessa hurt her, took away the armor of her age and her distance and turned her back into a little girl left on a doorstep.

And this is why I did my best to keep her out of our lives, he thought, his purpose reignited.

"I think so," he said. "For the time being. But

the good news is she doesn't have the jewels and she's given up on Margot having the jewels. So, hopefully this is the end."

"The end except that she's bribing pregnant women to get you out in alleyways and showing up at your charity fundraisers." Savannah shook her head. "I can't believe this."

Carter hesitated a moment before putting his hand over hers. "She seems…different, somehow. Defeated a little."

"Good," Savannah snapped and Carter flinched.

Savannah's eyes widened. "You're buying her act, Carter. She's suckering you in—"

He shook his head, denying it even as he knew that, in a way, it was true. This was his mother and stupidly, he wanted to believe her. "I don't think it's an act."

"That's how you know it's an act!" she cried. "Mom's a con! How can you forget that?"

"I'm not forgetting anything, trust me. I'm just saying she seems changed. She's broke. She owes people money. She's alone. I don't think she's a threat."

"Don't be a fool," Savannah whispered, her voice charging the silence that followed. Carter didn't have anything else to say, no words to justify the fact that he thought Vanessa was telling him the truth when she said she was out of angles.

Right now, he felt how much he wanted to believe Vanessa. Wanted to have a mother that wasn't going to use him for something. It made him nervous, since his entire life had revolved around keeping her away.

"What is this hold she has on you?" Savannah asked. "Ten years ago when you were her alibi in that breaking and entering case—?"

"What about it?" he asked, the sensation of sinking making him sick to his stomach.

"I just can't believe it—"

"Are you accusing me of lying?" he snapped, sounding guilty to his own ears. He glanced sideways at Zoe, who watched it all with her heart in her eyes.

"No, Carter," Savannah sighed. "I just don't understand and I want to. I really want to understand."

"There's nothing to understand. She was at my apartment the night of the break-in. Why she was there, I have no clue, she just was." His lies sounded cheap, and the silence his words fell into was so deep, so profound he thought they all might be drowning in it.

"I'm so sorry," Zoe breathed, sitting beside him looking slightly shell-shocked. Which, he supposed, was the right reaction when getting the greatest hits version of the Notorious O'Neills' exploits. "I should have kept my mouth shut."

Well, at least she got that right.

"No," Savannah said, sparking to life, "you did the right thing, because Carter never would have told me. Would you?"

He sat back, tired of dealing with this anger. "No," he said. "I wouldn't."

"Because you're still being the protective older brother—"

"No! Because what's the *point?*" He stood. "Look at you, Savvy. You've moved on. You're making a family. A new life. You don't need this crap."

"And you do?"

He was silent. The sounds of Katie's TV show in the living room tinkled through the kitchen door—where she was probably standing and eavesdropping, despite being told not to.

"She's why you weren't going to come back for Christmas, isn't it?"

"I'm busy," he said, through tight lips.

"You're an ass."

"It's really easy for you to judge me, Savvy, but everything I've done I have done to keep you guys safe. To keep her away from you."

"And I am telling you we are no longer kids. Tyler and I can take care of ourselves." Savannah stood and put her hands on his shoulders, her damp blue eyes a weight on his heart. "I would rather have you in my life," she said, "in Katie's life and the baby's life, even if it meant I had to deal with Mom."

"Last time you dealt with her she broke into your house, remember? Terrified you and Katie. Broke your heart all over again. That's what you want?"

"If it means I'd get my big brother back, then yes."

Carter didn't have anything else to say, no words to make the years somehow right. He rested his head against hers.

"He'll be there at Christmas," Zoe said, and Carter spun to face her as she clapped her hands over her mouth.

CHAPTER FOURTEEN

"WHAT ARE YOU DOING?" he asked.

"I'm sorry," she said, looking pained and uncomfortable. "But look at you guys. You need to be home for Christmas."

"This is my life, Zoe," he said, stunned at her audacity. "You can't speak for me."

"I know," she said and stood. "I know. You're right. And I've done enough. I've—" Her eyes, those big green eyes, met his and he saw too much. He saw her longing and her respect. Her sadness and her thousand-pound, happily-ever-after wishes. For all of them. "I've made a mess of things." Her laugh was sharp and awkward and Savannah flinched against him. "I told you that's the sort of thing I do. I'll—" she gestured toward the door "—leave. Thank you for the food and…" Her swallow was audible, her blush florescent. "Last night."

Her eyes clung to his again. "Thanks," she whispered and then she was gone. Out of the kitchen and through the living room.

Don't go after her, he told himself, willing his feet to be rooted to the kitchen floor. *You've done that already. It's her turn.*

His mind was a mess, everything in disarray. He needed some time to get things back in line and Zoe was counterproductive to all of that—it was better to give it some time, let both of them cool off. Let him get his life under control.

"Wait," he called and followed her, catching her at the front door, Katie's big blue eyes watching every move.

"You don't need to chase me down," Zoe said, turning away from the door. "You're off Prince Charming duty."

"It's not a duty, Zoe," he said, wondering if anything he'd said—anything that had happened in the past twenty-four hours—had mattered to her. He felt like the stuffing was being pulled out of his life. Chaos reigned and he was letting it happen because that was Zoe's natural habitat and he wanted her around.

But if she didn't want to be in his life, he wasn't about to beg.

"I'm going to let you call me," he said, and her eyes went wide.

"What?" she breathed.

"Normally after a night like last night, one

person has to call the other, and I think I'm going to let it be you."

"Thanks," she muttered.

"You know how I feel," he said with a shrug, as if it was casual when it felt anything but. When it felt like there was more on the line than there had ever been. He felt desperate and reckless, so out of control he couldn't even recognize himself.

There was a long pause and his heart, on ice for the last few years, wanted desperately to crawl back to the freezer.

He knew it. This tough, woman-in-control-of-her-life persona was just an act. In the end, she was too scared to try. Too unwilling—

"I'll call you," she said, and while he stood there, dumbstruck, she leaned in, kissed his lips and was out the door with a quick wave to Katie.

Sunlight poked holes through the dark corners of his life, and he turned to find his sister and niece staring at him with giant smiles across their faces. They shared a quick, laughing glance, and he didn't even care that they were laughing at him.

"We like her, Uncle Carter," Katie said, bouncing on his leather sofa.

"So do I," he agreed, rubbing the place on his chest where his heart beat so damn hard. "So do I."

MONDAY MORNING, Jim Blackwell opened his e-mail and felt a crack in the world open up around him. Angels sang. Heavenly light spilled across his desk and computer. Even Noelle Gilbert in the cubicle beside him looked less dour.

Carter O'Neill was holding a press conference on Wednesday night. There was not a question in Jim's mind that Carter was going to announce his candidacy for mayor in the 2011 primary.

A half hour later, when he got an e-mail notification that the mayor would be holding a press conference next week as well, Jim nearly did a jig.

Mayor-President Higgins was going to endorse the Golden Boy.

After the weekend Jim'd had, this was the kind of news to make a man want to sing. He'd applied some subtle pressure to the HR woman out at The Rouge about that blond dealer but he hadn't gotten anywhere.

It was beginning to feel as though this Carter O'Neill story was going nowhere, and his head hurt from beating it against a wall.

But now, with Carter all but cinching the Democratic ticket, *now* the rats would come out of the woodwork. They always did.

"Noelle," he said, and she turned her mousy

pointed nose toward him. "I'm in such a good mood, I think I'll let you buy me a coffee today."

"Go to hell, Blackwell," she sneered.

Ah well, Noelle wasn't feeling the love.

"Jim?" Tom said, wheeling his chair out around the edge of his cubicle. "You got a minute?"

Jim was even feeling okay about Tom. As okay about Tom as one could feel, so he said, "Absolutely," without any sarcasm.

"In the meeting room." Tom stood and walked over to the glass door of the big conference room.

"This about the press conference?" Jim asked, following Tom through the glass doors into the cool dark room. "Because I think—"

"I'm giving the press conference to Noelle."

"You're…what?"

"You're unglued, Jim. A loose cannon. I can't risk you in that press conference."

"But Noelle doesn't know the history. The angle."

"There is no angle. The only history is the stuff you've made up. You're off the story. We're going to put you on state politics."

"This is insane. I'm so close—"

"The head of HR out at The Rouge called this morning, Jim."

Jim rolled his eyes. "So what?"

"She called William."

Oh, he thought, something like worry creeping in. William was the editor in chief, and he had ties to The Rouge, protected that little cesspool like it was Baton Rouge's second coming.

"When you called to interrogate her this weekend, she thought you were doing a story on lax hiring practices, so when you hung up, she fired the blond dealer and put the pit boss on probation. After that, she called William to insist that there was nothing underhanded going on."

"The story isn't about The Rouge."

"I know that." Tom stood and stepped closer to where Jim was sitting. "I know that you don't think much of me, and I've let you get away with a lot because of the work you did last year—but enough is enough, Jim. You're leaving Carter O'Neill alone."

Jim sat back and stretched his arms up over his head, prepared to fight fire with fire. "And if I don't?"

Tom smiled, wide and bright like a kid on Christmas Day. "Then you're fired, Jim. I don't care about the awards you've won. You don't stop chasing windmills, and I will so happily—you have no idea how happily—shit-can you right back down to a weekly somewhere in Nebraska."

Tom stalked out, leaving Jim's good day and possibly his career decimated.

Jim's eyes narrowed.

You don't own me, he thought. *And you don't own this story.*

ZOE STROKED HER THUMB over the send button on her cell phone. One little push. Just a little tiny—

She pressed the button, her heart hammering in her throat. It was too late. She couldn't call him at eleven o'clock at night on a Monday. That was crazy. This whole thing was crazy.

She looked up at Carter's house, the windows alight, and felt like a sick, perverted stalker. That she had ginger cookies and salsa with her made it all a little worse.

"Hello?" he said after the second ring, and the rough/ smooth quality of his voice sent every internal muscle quivering.

I remember him! her body cried. *I remember and I want him back!*

"Anyone there?"

"Hi…ah…Carter," she said and winced. "It's Zoe."

His laugh was dark and rich, and she wanted to flop back on the ground and roll around in the sound of it.

"Hello, Zoe." His tone said he seemed to sense her discomfort and it made her smile. "How was your day?"

"Good," she said. "Great actually. I met with Eric Lafayette."

"And…"

"And, he's going to help me with the academy. Money, help finding the building," she paused, still feeling as if she were floating, and the meeting had been at noon. "Thank you, Carter."

"It wasn't me, Zoe. It was you. Congratulations."

"Thank you. And how about you? How was your day?" This would be a very normal conversation if she weren't outside his house, like a stalker. Maybe she should just leave. But she wanted so badly to see him.

Ever since leaving the Lafayette offices she'd been thinking of Carter and sharing this news with him. More than telling her mother or even Phillip, she had thought of Carter.

"Well, I've scheduled a press conference to announce my intentions to be mayor-president next term."

"Get out!" she gasped, and he laughed. "That's fantastic, Carter. Congrats!"

There was a long pause and Zoe looked up at the bright window. "Carter? Are you okay?"

"I think it's just my mom being back in town. And Blackwell is all over my ass in the papers. I can't make a single right move. I feel…"

"Trapped."

His laugh was a short little huff. "Exactly, Zoe. That's exactly how I feel. Let's meet for a coffee, or…" She heard him fumble with something. "I guess it might be too late?"

"No," she squeaked. She took a few steps to his door and rang his doorbell. "Not too late."

"Hold on a second. Someone's at my door." She heard him thumping toward the front door on the phone and wondered if she was going to die of embarrassment.

The door swung open and she held her breath, unprepared for the sight of him in sweatpants and a ratty Old Miss T-shirt. His feet were bare and they were probably the most handsome feet on the planet. Maybe the universe.

Yeah! her hormones cried. *Yeah for us!*

"Zoe!" he said, his smile bright and unguarded. He was truly happy to see her, and all her embarrassment fled the scene. Well, most of it—she still had a bagful of cookies and salsa to explain away.

He glanced down at his phone and shut it with a laugh. "This is great!"

"Are you sure? I was so excited about my day,

and it was so busy that by the time I thought of coming over here and celebrating with you, I didn't realize what time it was. And it's late. I mean…for me. But maybe for you, too. So anyway, we could do this another time—"

He pulled her into his house, right into his arms.

His kiss was sweet with just a little spice, and she sighed and melted right into him.

"I'm glad you're here," he whispered against her lips, his fingers sliding under the thin hem of her shirt and finding the sensitive skin of her side, her back, the curve of her hips.

"Me, too," she said, dropping her bag, cookies and all, so her hands could return the favor. Muscles jumped and twitched under her fingertips and the sweetness of the kisses was soon consumed by heat.

She kicked the door shut behind her and he laughed.

"How do you want to celebrate?" he asked, his hands sliding across her stomach up to her full, aching breasts.

"Take me into your bedroom and I'll show you."

AN HOUR LATER SHE GOT DOWN to revealing her dirty secret.

"You put the cookies in the salsa?" he asked.

They sat at his kitchen table wearing nothing but moonlight and smiles.

"Dip them, actually." She showed him then sighed with bliss. She didn't think it was possible, but they were even better after sex.

"You know you smelled like ginger cookies the first time I met you?" he said.

"When I stood on that chair?" she asked. "Really?"

He nodded and dipped one tiny piece of cookie in the salsa.

"Coward," she teased.

"Sweetheart, I mean you no offense, but there's no way this tastes good. I'm only humoring you out of my sincere gratitude for the filthy things you just did to me."

She blushed. They had been filthy. He bit into the cookie and grimaced. "Not good," he said. "At all." He took another bite, this time just of cookie. "But the cookies are great."

They ate in a silence so companionable, so rich with mutual affection, that she did something foolish.

"Do you like kids?" she blurted, and he stared, slightly dumbfounded, at her. "I mean, I guess I should know that, right? Unless, maybe you aren't thinking you'll be around or…whatever."

Yeah. That went well.

"I like kids a lot," he said solemnly. "I practically raised my brother and sister and even my grandmother is kind of a kid. And as for being around, I don't know, Zoe. Neither one of us does, but if something happens and we break up—it's not going to be because you're having a baby." He looked down at the salsa and cookies. "It might be because of your strange food addictions, but not because of the baby."

"Well, it won't be because of your mother, or your past, either," she said.

Carter was quiet for a second, taking a long time to chew, and she wondered if she'd said something wrong. "What about your mother?" he asked.

"Oh, well, trust me, if she had her way, we would never have started this. So, yes. In the end, she might be the straw that breaks your back." She tried to laugh, but found she couldn't. It was true. More true than she cared to admit.

"Mom's…ah…well, it's been the two of us our whole lives, and she's got some strong opinions on being a single mom and having relationships."

"So I'm not going to be meeting her anytime soon?"

"Not for as long as I can help it."

"Come on, in the battle of the mothers you're telling me yours is worse than mine?"

"My mom has this saying that she's been drilling into my head since I was a kid—"

"Eat your vegetables?"

She snorted. "I wish. No, she says, only pain is guaranteed."

"That's funny. My mother always said that trust is only rewarded with pain." Carter shrugged. "Maybe in the worst mother competition it's a tie."

"No, yours wins. Hands-down. Penny is a pain, but she stuck around," she whispered.

She kissed his hand and felt such warmth. Such lightness of being she could barely keep still.

"I know that we don't know everything about each other," she said, because she just could not shut up. "I have secrets, and from the conversation you had with your sister, I'm guessing you have some of your own."

"And?" he asked, but surprisingly the Carter O'Neill mask of displeasure didn't appear and it gave her courage to go on.

"And, if you want, you could tell me," she said.

"My secrets?" he asked.

"Yeah. Whatever it is your mom's got on you. Or—" she shrugged "—not. Either way, I just want you to know that I'll listen." He was quiet for a long time and she glanced up at him.

"I've never had friends," he said, shaking his head. "Growing up, I had only my brother and sister, and when I left Bonne Terre, I left them behind."

She swallowed a mouthful of cookie, the loneliness around him like a fog.

"I'll be your friend," she whispered.

"You already are," he said. The stool grated across the tile floor as he stood and approached her, his every muscle coiled and flexing in the moonlight. "And I'll tell you a secret, Zoe. Not all of them, but I'll tell you one right now."

His hands cupped her face and slowly slid down her neck, over her breasts, suddenly hot and heavy with a desire she thought had been satisfied. Her nipples hardened and she sighed with pleasure as his hands curved over the taut swell of her belly, feeling every contour of the sleeping baby inside.

"What's…ah…your secret?" she asked, her train of thought totally derailed.

"I didn't know this about myself," he said. "But I think I'm hot for pregnant women."

"We'll have to keep you away from Lamaze classes," she said, and the heat between them dissipated as they both laughed so hard they had to lean against each other.

"Zoe," he said. "This is really strange, but I'm so glad you stood up on that chair."

She leaned back, surprised and touched. Warmth filled her like sunshine on a hot day. "Me, too," she whispered. "Me, too."

The phone on the counter buzzed with an e-mail, ruining the mood, and she sat back, trying not to be irritated because he had warned her that he didn't turn the phone off for anyone.

But honestly, it was the middle of the night and she was naked.

Without batting an eye, Carter just reached over and held down the power button.

"What are you doing?" she asked.

"Turning it off. Whatever it is, it can wait until morning."

Well, she thought, letting him pull her from her chair and lead her back into the lush shadows of the back bedroom—as far as tokens of his affection, that one was hard to beat.

It was Thanksgiving and Carter had spent most of the day working from home, starting some campaign financing initiatives and looking over staff résumés that Amanda had forwarded him. He had the football game going on the TV in the corner, but by three o'clock he was done pretending that he wanted to work. Or even needed to.

He looked over the stuff on his desk and knew nothing was urgent.

The press conference yesterday had gone off without a hitch and already he'd gotten several calls of support. Eric Lafayette had come by the office with a giant check.

"We need more men like you working for this city," he'd said, and Carter's belief in himself, in the good he could do for Baton Rouge, had sky-rocketed. All those second thoughts brought on by his mother were gone.

Hell, even Blackwell was leaving him alone.

But now it was Thanksgiving Day, and there was nothing that needed to be done. He had a fridge full of Thanksgiving Day food but no one to share it with. He checked his watch—driving down to Bonne Terre now would get him there far too late for dinner, and besides, he didn't really want to see his family.

He wanted to see Zoe.

Zoe in the moonlight. Zoe laughing so hard salsa splattered out of her mouth. Zoe curled up beside him, the weight of that baby pressed against his hip.

Operating on instinct he packed up all the food, including the remaining sugar pie, and left his house. Zoe was going to be thrilled to see him, or maybe she'd be thrilled to see the sugar pie, but either way, this was the way he wanted to spend Thanksgiving.

In her gypsy camp.

He wouldn't even give her a hard time about the candles she would no doubt light.

His car lights flashed and the horn honked when he pressed the unlock button on his key ring.

"Hi, Carter," someone whispered, and he jumped out of his skin.

"Who—?"

His mother stepped out of the shadows beside his garage.

CHAPTER FIFTEEN

"CHRIST, MOM, YOU NEARLY gave me a heart attack!" he said.

"Sorry," she murmured, lingering in the hazy place between shadow and late-afternoon sunlight.

"How long have you been standing there?"

"Not long. I was about to go up and knock on your door."

"You okay?" He noticed that her lip was swollen and she held her hand against her chest as if it hurt. "What happened?"

"Nothing," she said, her smile quick and painful looking. "Nothing you need to worry about. I saw you on TV. Mayor, huh?"

"That's the plan," he said on a gust of breath. He wasn't impatient, he just didn't understand why she was here.

"Now that's a con," she said with a shake of her head. "Fundraising money alone would keep you in champagne—"

"It's not a con," he said, angry that she saw everything within those parameters. "I think I could do some good. I'm not sure you're familiar with the concept."

Her eyes were shadowed and the smile fled her face. Her lip looked painful, and he leaned closer to see her, but she backed farther into the shadows.

"What happened to your lip—"

"I'm fine. Trust me. I've had worse."

The silence dripped and simmered between them.

"How's work—" he said, just as she said, "So, it's Thanksgiving."

They laughed awkwardly.

"Work's…ah…fine. Good. Doing real good," she said. "Boss really likes me."

"That's great," he said, wondering if everything that came out of her mouth was a lie or just seemed like it.

"So, it's Thanksgiving," Vanessa said. "You going to Bonne Terre?"

"No," he said. "It's too late."

"You got a bunch of food," she said, looking down at the bag and Carter suddenly realized that his mother wanted them to share the holiday.

Like a regular family.

His stomach churned with horror and pity.

"I'm going to Zoe's," he said.

"Ah, right. Girlfriend." She smiled and he didn't deny the title, even though she clearly expected him to. "That's nice."

"Mom..." Unbelievably, he felt bad. He didn't understand how she did it, but he stood here feeling bad that the mother who'd deserted him years ago had no one to spend the holiday with.

"Don't worry, Carter. I understand. I'm not even sure why I came."

"I'd invite you, but she's not even expecting me."

"Well, I'm not quite the mother you bring to meet the girlfriend."

He laughed, but she didn't.

"Mom, are you okay? I mean, your lip? Do you need...help?"

"No. The last thing I need is help. I'm an O'Neill, remember? We take care of ourselves. I was just looking for company."

"Maybe..." He couldn't believe it as the words came out of his mouth, but they did, even though he knew his sister would kill him. "Another time?"

Her smile was brief, but it was the most sincere thing he'd ever seen on his mother's face. He suddenly remembered that before she'd left him with Margot and never looked back, this was the woman who had taken him to the pool. Put him to bed at night. Kissed his knees when he fell down.

The tenderness had been so easy to forget. He'd had to forget it, just to pull his family forward out of the abyss she'd dropped them into.

She retreated back into the shadows and he

opened his door, but then stopped. He had to tell her that this tie that bound them, this secret that had become a wall that separated him from every single thing he'd ever cared about, was about to be ripped away.

"I'm going to tell her," he said and he saw her turn, knowing immediately what he was talking about.

"The alibi?" she asked, and he could hear the disbelief in her voice.

He nodded.

"You sure that's smart? You have a lot at stake now."

He knew that, but he also knew that if he didn't tell Zoe, he'd lose her. Maybe not now, but at some point he'd freeze her out again, because this secret was ice in his veins. "What if she's spying?"

"She isn't. I know she isn't." End of discussion.

"You know, trusting people, sometimes—"

"You're a little late for motherly advice."

"Okay," she said, holding up her hands and he could see that two of her fingers were clearly broken. "Do what you have to do."

"Mom, what happened to your hand? This is crazy!"

"It's fine, Carter. Go to your girlfriend's. Have a nice time."

"Here," he said, reaching into the bag of food. "Take a sugar pie," he said. "I think Katie made it."

For a second something crumbled in her. All the support beams holding her up buckled and he saw an unfathomable pain that scratched at him.

"No thanks," she breathed.

And then she was gone.

"MOM, PLEASE, I AM BEGGING you to take the turkey out now!" Zoe cried, leaning against the counters in her own kitchen—a kitchen in which she was currently a stranger. But that's the way it was with Mom, she just took the space over. Made it hers.

"Sure," Penny said, emptying the potatoes Zoe had just mashed into a chipped china bowl that had come back from Houston with her. "I could take it out now and poison everyone."

"It won't actually poison us," Ben said, usually so calm but getting a little anxious about his organic, free-range, very expensive bird. Ben didn't know about Penny's take-no-prisoners Thanksgiving process. "I brined it first and it takes much less time to cook."

"You don't say?" Penny said, sprinkling cheese and green onions over the potatoes in a way that said she didn't care if he'd carried this bird to term and delivered it fully cooked—it wasn't coming out of the oven until Penny was ready.

"Wow," Ben breathed to Phillip, who only shrugged.

"Luckily her stuffing and cranberry sauce is amazing, so we won't starve," Phillip whispered.

The front door buzzed and Zoe pressed her intercom.

"Zoe?" Carter's disembodied voice floated through the speaker. Carter. Carter was on the other side of that door.

And her mother was on this side.

"You didn't tell me we were expecting someone else," Penny said, arching one eyebrow.

"We aren't," she said, taking a quick look over at Ben and Phillip. Ben shook his head no, but Phillip, who could almost always read Zoe's mind, was silently clapping.

This can't be happening, she thought, pressing the button to let him in.

A few moments later there was a light tapping on the door and she walked on numb feet to answer it. Having her mother and Carter in her apartment at the same time would be a Thanksgiving Day massacre.

She opened the door a crack and wedged herself into the opening. Carter glittered in late-afternoon sunlight, all shiny and golden, the most handsome man who'd ever stood on her doorstep, and Zoe's body sighed with fond memories.

"Hey," she said, nearly panting from the sudden stress.

"Hey, yourself!" He held up Savannah's bag of food. "I brought Thanksgiving—"

"Who is it, honey?" Penny yelled and Zoe winced.

"Oh." Carter's face fell. "You've got people over. Of course."

Oh, he was hurt. She could see it on his face and it was the last thing she wanted. "Please, Carter, it's not that I don't want you here—" *It's that I can't have you here.*

"Zoe? What are you doing?" The door was pulled out of her hand and she knew that she couldn't avoid this. She could only hope that whatever Carter felt for her would survive Penny's stubborn, protective love for her.

"This is my mom, Penny," Zoe said.

"Nice to meet you," Carter said, sticking out his hand, the perfect gentleman. Zoe wanted to tell him to run while he could, because her mom was going to eat him alive.

Penny shut right down, nothing but bricks behind her eyes.

"Humph," she said, looking him up and down as if he were roadkill before she walked away, yelling, "We don't have enough food," over her shoulder.

Zoe rested her head against the door, her

eyes shut. "I want you to come in, but if you do, there's a good chance that by the end of the night you'll never want to see me again." She lifted her head and looked him in the eye. "And I'm not exaggerating."

"I'm tough, Zoe. And what I feel for you is pretty tough, too."

Oh. Oh. Well, that was just the nicest thing anyone had ever said to her.

He capped it off by leaning forward and pressing a kiss to her cheek.

"Your mom doesn't scare me. Much," he whispered.

"In that case, come on in."

She opened the door to her home and her family, and it all felt better with him here. Warmer, brighter, a better place to be, and she really hoped he was right about the strength of his feelings. Because they were about to take a beating.

"I know I'm unexpected, but I come with food," he said, swinging the bag of food up onto a clear patch of counter. "Including sugar pie—it's sort of a family tradition."

"Oh, we know all about your family traditions, Carter O'Neill. I read the paper," Penny said, her look poisonous.

"Well you can't believe everything you read, Ms. Madison, but I will admit we're a colorful crowd.

And damn good cooks, especially my sister. Please make use of whatever you can."

Zoe had to admit, Carter was as smooth as a calm lake, and she exhaled the breath she'd been holding. She tucked her arm in his and turned him toward warmer waters.

"This is my friend Phillip and his partner, Ben—"

"Ben Grovener?" Carter asked, shaking Ben's hand. "I heard a rumor—"

"That I had died?" Ben joked. "Well, you know what Twain said—the rumors were greatly exaggerated."

Carter laughed appreciatively before replying, "No, I heard that you were back at work. That's fantastic." His enthusiasm was sincere and it made her like him even more, as if that were possible. "How are you feeling?"

"Like I was hit by a car, but every day is better than the last, so I can't complain." Ben poured Carter a glass of wine from one of the three bottles that Phillip had brought. "And you, running for mayor, that's good news for this city."

"Well, I hope so," Carter said, taking the glass. Zoe shared a long look with Phillip.

"We can double-date now," Phillip whispered, and Zoe smiled, happiness building up inside her like champagne bubbles.

"I have some big plans," Carter said, "some

neighborhood initiatives and some ideas that I think would help us bring in more national conferences and tourism…" Carter trailed off and smiled, embarrassed, and Zoe just wanted to curl him up and put him in her pocket, he was so sweet. "I've been alone working all day," he said. "I'm afraid I can't quite shut up."

"Don't shut up on my account," Ben said. "The truth is…" He glanced back at Phillip, who only shrugged.

"It's your life, sweetie," Phillip said. "You gotta do what you gotta do."

"The truth is, I would love to hear more about your ideas in an official capacity," Ben said.

Carter's eyebrows elevated. "If that's you asking for a job, you're hired. You're a fighter, Ben, and I have admired your work for a long time. I know you're active in the state building, but if you're interested in city politics, I'd love to have you on my team."

Ben blinked and Zoe rocked back while Phillip stroked Ben's shoulder, the most colorful political wife the city had ever seen. "I'll call on Monday," Ben said. "We can talk more then."

"I look forward to it," Carter said and took a sip of wine before turning to Zoe.

"Look at you," she said, cupping her hands over his elbows and giving him a little shake and a squeeze. "Handing out jobs and sugar pie—you're going to be a great mayor."

"Well, I'm not there yet," he said, but Zoe leaned in to kiss him anyway. Mayor or not, she was totally smitten. Those little seeds of attraction and affection were growing into some foreign flower, an exotic plant that felt a lot like love.

And she wasn't scared. Standing there on the high wire of her life, she wasn't scared of her feelings for this man she hardly knew.

And maybe that should concern her, but she simply couldn't work up the energy.

The slam of the oven door and the crash of a roasting pan hitting the counter snapped Zoe away from Carter.

"Mom, you okay?" she asked, but the second she got a look at her mother's face, she knew what was coming.

"I'm fine," her mother snapped. "But you need to get your head examined."

"Uh-oh," Phillip muttered.

"Mom," Zoe begged. "Please, don't—"

"Am I supposed to sit idly by while you pretend you're not having a baby? While you run around acting like you have no responsibilities to anyone but yourself?"

"I'm not pretending anything," she said, forcing herself to keep her cool and not rise to this old and tired bait. "I'm living my life and enjoying myself—"

"And how much are you going to be enjoying yourself when you're raising a baby all by yourself, you're exhausted and stressed out, and this man is nowhere to be seen?"

"You don't know that's going to happen."

"Oh, please, Zoe. You never could be realistic. You're going to be a single mother. Now is not the time—"

"Then *when?*" Zoe cried, her cool bolting away from her. "Look at you, Mom—you're sixty years old and you've never had a relationship."

"I have you—"

Zoe took a deep breath and realized that Phillip and Ben had grabbed their coats and were headed to the door.

"No," she cried, heartbroken to see her holiday falling to pieces. "Don't leave."

"I'll call you later," Phillip said. "You get this hashed out with your mom. Get it dealt with for good."

Ben and Carter exchanged manly nods and then her friends were gone.

"Look at what you've done, Mom! You chased them away."

"Well, I'm sorry about that. I am, but honestly, honey, I can't watch you get hurt like this."

"I'm not hurt!" she cried. "I'm happy. I'm so happy."

"You're going to have a baby," her mother said, as if it were a death sentence, and Zoe wondered, not for the first time, how hard it had been for Penny to be a single mother at twenty.

Much harder than what Zoe was about to face, being thirty-seven and ready for a family. Eager for one.

"Ms. Madison," Carter said, and Penny turned her furious eyes on him. "I know you don't know me, and I understand that the way Zoe and I got together would concern any mother—"

"Don't try and smooth talk me," Penny said. "You're slick, but I can see right through you. She's broke, you know. Teaching dance classes without insurance. No savings."

"I just got funding for the academy—"

"Right, a new dance school and a new baby. You can guess who will be looking after this child."

"I want to help. I'm sure Phillip does, too," Carter said.

"Sure," Penny practically snarled. "Where are you going to be in five months, when she's fat and has cracked nipples and can't stop crying?"

"Please, God, just kill me now," Zoe whispered, but Carter reached over and took her hand.

"I know she's having a baby," he said. "I'm excited for her. For me, and for whatever part I have in her life at that time. It doesn't put me off, or scare me."

"Well it should," Penny snapped. "You should both be scared."

"No!" Zoe cried. "I should be happy. I should be thrilled. I'm having a baby, not serving jail time or enduring hardship. I'm bringing joy into my life."

"Well," Penny said, pursing her lips. "It seems to me your constant search for joy is what got you into this mess."

Oh. Oh wow. Had her mom just called her a joy-seeking slut? She glanced over at Carter, who was staring back at her.

"I'm inspired by your constant search for joy," he whispered.

Sweet man. Whatever happened with him, she would not regret it. Not for a minute.

"Mom," she breathed, "you've failed to realize that I am all grown-up. I'm a thirty-seven-year-old woman. And I'm sorry you had me before you were ready. I'm sorry that life was so hard on you, but this was a decision I made."

"A decision after a mistake. An accident. I know all about it, sweetheart. I've been there."

Something snapped in her head and anger flooded her, filling her hands and her feet, coursing through her veins and siphoning through her lungs. She realized that by keeping her baby's conception a secret, she was damning her daughter to the same relationship with Penny she'd had to live with. The same strange prison of love and resentment.

And she wouldn't do it. Couldn't do it.

Her mother's instinct roared to life, overshadowing the bond she had with her own mother, already stretched thin and worn down.

"Mom, there's something you need to know." The tone of her voice, dark and loud, made both Carter and Penny turn to face her. Part of her recognized that this was her last secret from Carter. After this, she was just an open book, while he was still a mystery to her in so many ways. But she wasn't about to tell him to leave.

"This baby was a decision," she said, and Penny opened her mouth to say something, but Zoe smacked her hand down on the counter. "Let me talk. All my life I've let you say these poisonous things, these hurtful things, and I'm done. You won't do it anymore. Not to me and never, ever to this baby."

"I never meant to hurt you," Penny whispered, her eyes wide, and Zoe knew that her mother was telling the truth. She just didn't know how to be any other way—her years of sacrifice for Zoe had worn her down to a blunt object with no finesse. No empathy.

But with a baby coming, things needed to change.

"That doesn't make it okay anymore. You need to know." She looked over at Carter, who was steadfast and serious, watching her every move. Her every breath. "Maybe both of you do. I was pregnant about a year and a half ago." Penny exhaled hard and slumped against the counter. "I was dating a violin player in the orchestra and... it just happened. It wasn't planned, but it wasn't a mistake." The word was a barb she threw right at her mother.

"I was thrilled. Delirious. Victor, not so much. When I...miscarried—" the lump in her throat, the sudden tears were a surprise but she rolled over them, undeterred "—Victor was relieved. I broke up with him, and as months passed, I realized that I wanted a family. A baby. My baby. And I knew that I could wait for another man to come along and make this happen for me, or I could do it myself."

Oddly, she wasn't looking at her mother. She watched Carter, told Carter. She watched her words, the words she'd never said out loud, sink in.

"What are you saying?" Penny asked.

Zoe ran her hands over her belly.

Sorry, baby, she thought, because she was breaking her promise. But she realized that her promise was just a different kind of jail than the one her mother put her in, but a jail nonetheless, with its own walls and locks. And, she thought, glancing at Carter, maybe she'd kept this secret out of embarrassment, and she didn't want to be embarrassed about her child. About wanting a child.

She was proud, and it was time for this to end.

"The baby's father is sample 1371D."

CHAPTER SIXTEEN

THE SILENCE FILLED THE ROOM until the pressure in the air was so thick, so ominous, her head hurt. But Zoe pressed on.

"He's tall, but not too tall. Brown hair, blue eyes. No history of cancer or heart disease. He's a student at U of T—a double major in biomedicine and earth science." She started to babble out of sheer nerves. "I wanted someone good at math and science, you know, who would balance me out."

"Of course," Carter said, sincere and earnest, not a hint of mockery in his voice or face. Nothing but…pride. Affection. "That makes sense, Zoe. Perfect sense."

"Are you saying you went to a sperm bank?" Penny asked, her face creased in horror and confusion. "You…did this on purpose?"

"I wanted a family, Mom."

"I'm your family."

"You're my… I don't know, jail cell. And I'm yours. You love me, but you resent me. And I love you, I do. But I sure as hell am beginning to resent you."

"Resent me?" Penny whispered, her eyes welling up with tears, and Zoe felt awful. Really awful. But there was nothing she could do. These walls needed to be broken down so that something new could be built.

"I don't know what to say," Penny whispered, folding up a tea towel into precise corners. "I think…maybe…" She sighed and looked around at the turkey and the potatoes growing cold on the counter. "I'm going to leave."

It was on the tip of Zoe's tongue to stop her, to tell her it was okay, to wipe all of this away, but Carter reached over and twined his fingers with hers, gathering them all up until their palms were pressed together. Tight. She felt his heart beating in the center of his hand, just as she felt the beat of the baby's heart in her belly like the flutter of a small bird, the tide of an ocean…of life.

Family, she thought, knowing it was true no matter how unlikely.

This man, the baby, her. That was family.

"I'll call you in a few days, Mom," Zoe said, as good a compromise as she could come up with. She walked toward the door where her mother stood, gathering her things. "Do you want to take some food?" she asked quietly, but Penny shook her head.

When she looked up, her mother's green eyes, so familiar, so much a part of her life and her memories, were wide and wet with tears. "I never meant to be this way," Penny whispered. "The last thing I ever wanted to do was hurt you."

"I know," Zoe whispered.

"And I don't want you to be hurt now," she said, still managing to shoot a sharp look over Zoe's shoulder at Carter, and Zoe fought a smile. Good old Penny Madison—she took a beating but kept on swinging.

"I'm a big girl," Zoe said. "A woman with my own life. I can take care of myself and my baby."

Penny cupped Zoe's face, a tender touch. "You were always so dreamy," Penny said. "So lost in your own little world and I…I guess I am just used to worrying. I'm sorry," she said, wrapping Zoe's once-favorite scarf around her neck as she walked out.

Zoe shut the door behind her and rested her head against it, wondering if Carter was going to leave, too. If maybe this was all just a little too much for him.

It was way too much for her and it was her life.

"I wouldn't blame you if you wanted to leave," she said, talking to the door.

His hand stroked her back, a warm touch through the cowboy shirt with the lassoing hearts she almost wore on their first fake date.

Funny, she'd known this guy less than a month,

but his mark was like a thick bold tick on her time line. Her whole life was split into halves—before Carter and after Carter.

"Can I tell you something?" he asked, his voice in her ear, his breath a warm breeze on her neck that made her skin do a shimmy.

"Please," she said, "the more embarrassing the better."

"I'm proud of you," he said, still rubbing her back, and she almost started to cry. All the emotions of the day welled up and nearly drowned her, but she pressed her head hard into the door, the pain barely keeping the tears at bay. "I'm proud to be in your life."

She waited for the but. The "but I'm going to be mayor, and you're way too nuts to have kicking around City Hall."

It never came.

His hands kept making those wide warm circles on her back, drugging her, and suddenly she found a lot of courage, enough courage to do stupid things. But in for a penny, in for a pound, was pretty much how Zoe operated.

She turned, wiping away the tears that clung to her eyelashes. "What if I told you I was falling in love with you?" she asked. His eyes got wide and he stepped back, his shoulders slumping slightly as if she'd just punched her in the gut. "I'm not saying I'm there, but it's not far off. You still want to be in my life?"

As he stood silent and stared at her, Zoe died, over and over again, and wondered if spontaneous combustion really happened.

"I've…ah…turned away from love a lot in my life, for a lot of stupid reasons," he finally said, his fingers reaching for hers, and she couldn't help reaching out for him. "I don't want to do it anymore.

"But there's something you need to know about me," he said. "Something that might change your mind."

"Are you donor 1371D?" she asked, making a joke because he was suddenly so serious, sucking all the air and light out of the world. "Because that would be weird," she finished lamely.

His smile was cockeyed and distant. "You know about my family," he said.

"The Notorious O'Neills," she said. "Don't tell me there's more—a grandfather in the mafia or something."

"No," he said and then paused. "Although, maybe."

"Carter—" she laughed.

"It's me," he said. "It's about me. About what I've done." His fingers became stiff in her hands, and she squeezed them, feeling suddenly like despite the fact that he was standing right in front of her, he wasn't really present.

"It can't be that bad," she whispered.

"I lied in court," he said. "For my mother. I gave her an alibi ten years ago so she wouldn't go to jail."

Zoe's jaw dropped open. *"You?"* It was like hearing Smokey the Bear admit to being an arsonist.

"Me. She said if I didn't do it, she would go back to Bonne Terre and ask my sister. Or my brother. And I knew...God, I knew my sister would do it. Savvy was so desperate to have her mother back, she would have done anything. So I lied, in court, but I made her promise that she'd never bother Savannah or Tyler again. Ever. Not that she honored the agreement, but at the time I thought I was protecting my family."

"Of course," she said, able to see every bit of convoluted logic. "You were doing what you thought was best."

"I've been doing what I thought was best ever since. I thought that if she came back to me once, she'd come back again, so I stayed away." He shook his head, looking so lost and alone it broke her heart. "I stayed away from my family and my home and I've been lying ever since. Everything I've done..." He shrugged. "It's all been a lie."

"No," she sighed, cupping his face in her hands, holding on to him as hard as she could as if pushing the truth—the truth of him as she saw it—right into his skull. "No, it hasn't. Wanting to do good, wanting to help this city, even staying away from your family to protect them—that's you. That's who you are."

"Not a liar?" he asked, his laugh thick with scorn, and there was a terrible desperation in the sound. "A criminal? Just another Notorious O'Neill, despite every effort I've made to be something else?"

"Oh, no," she sighed. "You're a good man, no matter what your last name is."

His smile was tender, like early-morning sunshine, and he ran his fingers through her hair, tugging a little at the ends. "And you are going to be a good mother."

She laughed, feeling as if she'd stepped off a bridge. It wasn't air beneath her, but it wasn't the ground, either, and it was going to take some serious getting used to.

"So," he said, looking around her kitchen at the dinner that was intended to feed four with leftovers for a week. The air was thick with the smell of garlic and turkey. Sweet potatoes and cranberries. His grin was wicked and knowing. "What are we going to do with all this food?"

"Eat," she said, putting her arms around his waist, reaching up to kiss those beautiful lips. "But not just yet."

JIM BLACKWELL LIFTED his finger and within moments another shot of Beam was at his elbow. Drinking in the day got you much better service. Much better. Maybe he should write a story about that—the benefits of daytime boozing.

"You mind putting on the mayor's press conference?" Jim asked the brunette behind the bar who looked like she'd been tending bar for about twenty lifetimes.

She glanced back at the soap opera flickering on the TV above the bar and sighed as she reached up and turned the knob until Mayor-President Higgins's face filled the screen. The old man was about to endorse Mayor Pro Tem Carter O'Neill for mayor, and Jim was sitting in a bar.

Off the story. Off the goddamned story. And who knew Noelle was so uncrackable, unbribeable. Maybe he should have been nicer to her before he'd needed a favor.

Ah. Hell.

The bourbon burned on the way down.

"Jim Blackwell." The soft purr of a woman's voice was a very welcome distraction from his own sad life.

"Hello there," he said, swiveling on his chair and nearly falling off it when he saw who it was.

The blonde that had to be Carter O'Neill's mother. The HR bitch out at The Rouge hadn't confirmed it, but this was the same femme fatale who'd been in that alley with Carter.

He blamed it on the booze, but he could only gape as she sat next to him and ordered a Diet Coke.

"Stop staring," she muttered, not once glancing over at him. "You look like an idiot."

"How…how did you find me?"

"You've been drinking here every day for the last three days," she said. "You're hardly incognito."

"What are you doing here?" he asked, unable to contain his delight at the story coming back to him like a lost child.

She stared down at the ice cubes melting in her glass for a long time, and he decided he needed to nudge her along.

"You're Vanessa O'Neill, aren't you?" he asked, and she nodded, finally taking a sip from the thin red straw.

"You're here about your son?" he asked, leading her down the only path he wanted her to go.

She took a deep breath, like a reluctant diver on the high board, then spun to face him. "I have information," she said. "On him."

Oh. Oh, this was better even than he thought. She was going to sell him out.

"Okay, I'm listening."

She shook her head. "It's going to cost you."

He licked his teeth, trying not to look too eager. Trying not to pump his fists in the air, do a victory lap around the bar. "How much?"

"Ten thousand," she whispered, looking down at the bar, her fingers spread wide. Two of them were taped together and the dots connected in his head.

"That's enough to get you out of the country," he said.

She was silent, strung so tight she was about to snap, and while he didn't enjoy her misery, he was real glad it had brought her to his door. Or bar, as it were.

"That's a lot of money," he said. It was going to wipe out his savings. But what was he saving it for, really?

"What I have to tell you will ruin his career," she said, lifting burning eyes.

Oh, it was so sweet.

"Ten thousand," he agreed, pushing away his glass of bourbon. "Now, what's your story?"

CHAPTER SEVENTEEN

THE ROARING IN CARTER'S ears was the sound of his life coming down around him. Everything he'd worked for—law school, city council, Mayor Pro Tempore—it crashed and crumbled, obliterating itself into dust. Into nothing.

"This is an attack!" Amanda cried, pacing in front of the big windows of the mayor's golden oak office. Carter sat in a vacuum, a million miles away from these people and these events.

But the ripped and torn sensation of betrayal he felt, he felt down to his bones. He could barely breathe.

Mayor Pro Tempore Lies in Court.

That was the headline Monday morning. Not nearly as catching as Deputy Deadbeat Daddy, but it got the job done.

"He names one source," Amanda said. "One *anonymous* source. I can't even believe they published such crap."

"You need to get a statement together, and fast," Ben Grovener said. Poor Ben, who just happened to be the right lawyer at the wrong time, had been sitting outside Carter's office when the story broke.

"We can destroy Blackwell," Amanda snarled. "No doubt about it, he paid someone. For sure he paid someone to tell this story."

The story. With one anonymous source. One anonymous female source. This secret had been buried for ten years, and four days after he tells Zoe, this happens? He didn't want to believe it, but could he believe anything else?

The roar in his ears was deafening. The pain in his chest made him sick.

The only other option was that his mother had betrayed him again, but he didn't want to believe it. The kid, that stupid kid that still lived in him, wanted to howl that it wasn't her. That it couldn't have been her. She wasn't conning him. She'd told him there was no angle.

Which only left Zoe. Broke, about-to-have-a-baby Zoe.

Christ. Everywhere he turned it hurt. He breathed hard through his nose, trying to numb himself to this pain.

"With the right spin, you can control this," Ben said. "But you need to act fast. Something aggressive, but that takes the high road. Carter?" Everyone in the room turned to him, waited for him to get to his feet and start fighting. Start giving out orders and putting together a plan. "Carter?" Ben asked, glancing quickly around the room and then back at Carter. "I know this is a shock, but we—"

"It's true," Carter said, his voice a broken rasp.

The mayor swiveled in his seat, shock clear on his face.

Carter looked right into his mentor's eyes and gave up the fight. There was nowhere left to hide. "I lied in court to keep my mother out of jail. It doesn't matter if Blackwell paid someone, or the source is anonymous. It's true."

"Oh, my God," Amanda sighed, collapsing onto the stiff couch in the corner.

"I'm sorry," Carter said, knowing how hard Amanda had worked on his behalf.

"You'll be disbarred," Ben said, and Carter nodded. "And the mayoral race—"

"It's over," Carter said. And it had been torn from him, just as he was beginning to taste the rest of his life. Sweet after a lifetime of sour.

He was light-headed with anger and pain.

"Well, Christ, son, if you'd told us we could have dealt with it," Mayor Higgins said.

"How?" Amanda cried. "He lied. In court. To protect his criminal mother from further jail time. There's no good way to spin this."

"She's right," Carter said, the blunt truth of the situation pushing him into action. He turned all that anger he felt back on himself. Nobody had done this to him; he'd done it to himself. After all those years of worrying that his family would be his downfall, in the end it was just him and his mistakes. "I'm not going to confirm or deny the story. But I am going to withdraw from the primary."

"You might as well just say it's true," Ben said. "That's what everyone is going to think. And you're still going to get disbarred."

"I know," he said. "But it gets me out of here faster."

And out is what he needed. A thousand miles between him and Baton Rouge and Jim Blackwell and Zoe, was what he needed. He needed time to get himself under control and to think this all through, because right now he was scared of what he would say—how his pain might find its way free.

"I'm sorry," he said for the last time. "It's been a pleasure to work with you." He glanced at Ben. "And it would have been a pleasure to work with you."

And then he left, walking down the long hallway from the mayor's office to his own office as mayor pro tempore for the very last time, as if he was marching to his death.

The chill he'd tried to purge from his veins, the cold he'd thought Zoe had thawed was back, but tenfold, encasing him in ice. He could barely walk, barely think past his anger. His self-disgust.

"Mr. O'Neill?" Gloria said, as he put his hand to the knob on his closed office door.

"What?" he snapped and she flinched.

God, he was sorry about that too. *How many apologies,* he thought, *will make my life okay? How many times do I need to whip myself for what I've done?* He'd paid his whole life for every decision he'd ever made and it clearly hadn't been enough.

"Zoe Madison is in there—"

Ice filled his brain and his anger was frigid. His control complete. Zoe had distracted him from his diligent command over his life and secrets. She'd been the key that had unleashed everything.

Foolishly, he'd thought it was a good thing, that her affection and love was something that might heal him. Fix him.

But he was an O'Neill. And he was broken down to his DNA.

He pushed open the door and the sight of her jumping out of a chair, a copy of the paper crumbled up in her little hands, was like an ice pick right to his heart.

It hurt to see her. To smell the spicy ginger cookie scent of her.

"Carter?" she cried, racing around the table. "Are you okay? I saw the paper and—"

"I'm fine."

She stilled, her eyes wary, her fingers fumbling with the paper. "Fine?" she whispered. "But the paper…"

"What do you want me to say, Zoe? I'm going to be disbarred, I'm dropping out of the mayoral race and I've been disgraced on the front page of the paper. Again." His phone buzzed and he scrolled down the list of e-mails he'd gotten in the past ten minutes. Endless. His career was going to go down in a barrage of e-mails.

"What are you doing?" she whispered, the pain like a wind blowing right out of her.

"Answering e-mails," he said without looking at her, doing his best to freeze her out.

"Put that away!" she snapped. "Talk to me!"

"I have work to do, Zoe."

"Why are you acting like this?"

"Could you be more specific?"

"Like it doesn't matter!" she cried. "Like you're made out of ice."

"You'll have to forgive me," he said, "I wasn't aware there was a protocol."

"Carter!" she cried, and slapped the phone out of his hand. It hit the wall and skidded across the carpet.

"That was unnecessary," he said.

"Are you…are you mad at me? Do you think…"

"That you are the anonymous source?" His anger surged and his vision went black. "It had occurred to me. Seems a pretty incredible coincidence that I keep this secret for ten years and the week after I tell you it's all over the paper. You sold me out once, Zoe, and your mother made it very clear that you're broke. Information like this must come with a pretty attractive price tag."

She gasped, swallowed hard as if she might throw up, and he just stared at her. Watched her like she was a stranger, and maybe she was. In the end, maybe they were all just strangers. Love, intimacy, family, they were shams, fake oases for the desperate. And oh, God, that had been him, hadn't it? Desperate for someone to hold him, to listen to his secrets, to forgive him of his crimes.

Pathetic.

Suddenly, he felt sick.

"I get that you're mad, Carter. But it wasn't me." She reached out for him; her fingers, those hands he adored so much reached for him, and he stepped away, the idea of being touched unbearable. His life—the life that her touch had illuminated, brought into focus—was over. Shattered. "Your mother—"

Of course it was his mother.

With her words, the knowledge settled around him like a winter fog. He could strike out at Zoe all he wanted, but he knew, had always known, it couldn't have been her. Could never have been her.

But his mother had all the practice in the world at breaking his life into pieces.

And now that he was clearheaded about it, the clues all fell into place. The broken fingers. The split lip. She'd sold him out to save herself—he should have seen it coming, but he'd been too drunk on Zoe, on love and trust and belonging to someone. Belonging with someone. God, what a disaster. His mother had been right, trust was only rewarded with pain. Well, not again. Never again would he be blindsided like this.

"It doesn't matter." That was the truth. Nothing mattered. The chill did its job and he was totally numb. "Nothing matters, Zoe. It was only a matter of time."

"Please don't freeze me out, Carter," she whispered. This time he couldn't brush off her hands, and they touched his face, blazes of heat against his skin. Her fingers stroked his lips, his cheeks, and it felt so good, so unbelievably good that he couldn't push her away. "Why are you doing this to us? To what we have?"

"What we have?" he asked, his laughter a weapon he used against both of them, a sword slicing them both in half. "We met a month ago. You stood on a chair and accused me of getting you pregnant. We went on a date and I got humiliated in front of the entire city, which frankly was a trend that continued. You are having a baby. I have no career and we—" he touched her chest and she flinched "—don't have anything," he finished.

She gasped and reeled back slightly before shaking her head, determination clear on her little elfin face. He should have known she would fight him. He should have known she would make this hard. "I don't believe you," she whispered.

"It doesn't matter what you believe," he said. "It's over."

"I could be there for you," she said, her hands on his chest, tears in her beautiful eyes. "I could help."

"I don't need help." He grabbed her hands in one of his, lifting them from his chest. It was time to say goodbye and end this right now. He squeezed her wrists and gave them a little shake, ignoring the tears in her eyes, the quiver of her lip—all the terrible, terrible pain he was causing her. "I'm an O'Neill, and we take care of ourselves."

ZOE LEFT CARTER'S OFFICE and tried hard not to run. She felt every eye on her and knew that they all thought that she was the anonymous source. Insane. Everyone was insane. The world had turned upside down. She'd gone to bed last night like she had every night since Thanksgiving, thinking about love and family, and she woke up this morning to find out how disposable she was.

Her stomach lurched, and she detoured to the bathroom off the big marble foyer on the first floor.

She hadn't thrown up since the eleventh week of her pregnancy, but now her stomach was in her throat. She pushed opened the door of the first stall so hard it bounced back against the metal frame and the bang rang out like a shotgun blast. Her fingers shook as she shut the door behind her, fumbled with the metal clasp and finally just gave up, pressing her hot cheeks against the cool metal.

How had she been so wrong? So damn wrong?

Her mother had been right. The only thing guaranteed was pain. She sank down on the toilet and stuffed her fist in her mouth so no one could hear her crying.

THE WEEK DRAGGED BEHIND Zoe like deadweight. Every minute, even the good ones, were tests to endure. She'd thrown herself into her work for the academy, building her future, meeting by meeting. Handshake by handshake. Eric Lafayette had been wildly helpful, but the joy had barely registered. She was swaddled in cotton, insulated against every sensation. Even the pain had become a dull throb.

Zoe punched the numbers into the lockbox outside the little storefront off St. Louis and pulled out the key.

Dusk fell in grey slabs through the windows and she turned on the lights. It was dusty and smallish. It needed paint and some water damage in the back corner had to be repaired.

But—she spun—mirrors along the west wall. A barre. Dressing rooms in the back. The price was right, thanks to a loan from the bank and Eric's help. The neighborhood wasn't great, but it was changing—

The front door clicked and the room's pressure changed. Her heart leaped into her throat; her hand flew to her Mace.

"Who's there?" she yelled, scared half to death, but hoping in some stupid place in her heart that it was Carter.

"Sorry, sweetie." Penny stepped in through the

foyer, her red raincoat a smudge of color in the gray. "I hope I didn't frighten you."

Zoe nearly blacked out with relief. She sagged against a cement pillar.

"Jeez, Mom, you could have called or something. How did you know where I was?"

"Phillip," she said, looking down at her fingers before tucking them into her pockets. "He does a good job of keeping tabs on you."

She hadn't talked to her mother since Thanksgiving, though Penny had called after Carter had resigned from his job. Zoe hadn't answered, not ready to swallow her mother's righteousness.

"Well, you found me," Zoe said. "What do you think?"

Penny looked around. "Is this for the academy? It's such a big step. Can you afford—" Penny stopped midsentence and Zoe fumed, wondering if her mother was ever going to change. Was ever going to treat her like an adult. "I'm sorry," Penny said, and Zoe held her breath, getting the sense that her mother was apologizing for more than just that comment.

"I'm sorry for the way I've acted, and the way I reacted to your baby. I think that in all my fear for you, I never once told you how excited I am. And what a good mother I think you'll be."

"Thank you," Zoe breathed, flattered beyond measure.

"About Carter—"

"You can say *I told you so,* if you want," Zoe said, her heart so tired and sore she couldn't even say his name. "You were right. He's left."

"I'm not here to say *I told you so,*" Penny said. "I'm not here to make this pain worse."

To Zoe's utter amazement, Penny's eyes filled with tears. "You're so brave, Zoe. So much braver than me."

Zoe stepped forward and reached for her mother's hands. "That's not true, Mom. You were twenty. A kid—"

Penny shook her head. "I'm not talking about being a mother. I'm talking about…" She sighed heavily. "I don't know, being a woman. Being a lover or a girlfriend. You throw your heart around like it can't be broken. You've always done that."

Zoe rested her head against her mother's shoulder. Her broken heart pounded and throbbed in her chest, proving what a reckless mistake that had been.

"I had relationships, you know," Mom said, and Zoe lifted her head, slightly scandalized.

"What?"

"Boyfriends over the years. I just never cared enough about any of them to bring them home to

you. Or maybe I just cared so much about you…"
She stopped. "Either way, I think…now, I think
that was a mistake. I should have opened our world,
even if there had been some pain involved."

Zoe laughed. "No, Mom, you were right. This
pain…" She touched her chest, rubbed at the sore
spot as if it might help. "Nothing is worth this
pain. I thought I would never regret what Carter
and I had, but I was wrong. I wish I'd never stood
on that damn chair."

"Oh, honey," Penny said. She folded Zoe in a
tight hug, and Zoe was ready to go back to that
world. The world of the two of them, insulated
against everybody else. And her mom could make
that happen. Things were safe with her mom; no
one got in and no one got hurt.

"You don't mean that," Penny said.

"I do, Mom. I do. Carter…that was a mistake."

Penny blinked and stroked Zoe's face. "No,
honey, a mistake is not trying. A mistake is never
opening the door to the possibility of love. Don't
let this pain change you like it changed me."

Zoe's phone buzzed in the pocket of her raincoat
and she fished it out, her heart hammering hard in
her chest. Sure, she could talk a good game about
regretting Carter, but she wished it was him on
that phone. Longed to hear his voice.

"Hello?" she said.

"Zoe, sorry to bother you, but this is Savannah Woods...O'Neill. This is Carter's sister."

"Savannah, hi," she said, surprised. "How did you get this number?"

"I'm so sorry. This is illegal in a bunch of different ways I'm sure, but my sister-in-law has friends in law enforcement and I would never have done this, but we're having an emergency."

"Emergency? Are you okay?"

"Fine. But we can't find Carter."

CHAPTER EIGHTEEN

ZOE STOOD OUTSIDE CARTER'S dark condo with his spare key in her hand. He'd shown her where it was a week ago. God, had that been last week? It felt like a lifetime ago.

If she used this key and he was in there, he was going to lose his mind. Rightly so, she had to admit, but he wasn't answering his cell phone. Savannah had talked to him briefly, a few days ago, right after the news had broken. He'd said he was going after Vanessa, but after that, five days of silence. And going after Vanessa—that could mean anything. New Orleans. New York. Hell, he could be in Beijing.

Savannah had called the police and hospitals, but neither had any information. She'd tried his assistant, even the mayor's office, but no one had talked to him in a week. Zoe called Eric Lafayette, who said Carter had just disappeared off the face of the earth.

There was a good chance he was just holed up in his condo. Lying low. But enough was enough, she thought, sliding the key in the lock—people were freaking out.

Not her, of course, she told herself. She didn't care. Since there was nothing between them, why would she care? But her hands were sweating, and she really, really hoped he was in there, maybe drunk. Hungover. She'd even take him angry.

But please, she prayed, let him be safe.

"Hello?" she cried, stepping into the dark foyer. His running shoes were there, the iPod still in them. She kicked over a pile of mail from the mail slot, which made her nervous. He hadn't been here to move it. "Carter?" she cried.

She ran through the rooms but it only confirmed what she knew.

Carter was gone.

Carter was gone, and no matter how much she pretended she didn't care, it was a lie.

Love was alive in her.

She called Ben and Phillip and then her mother.

And then her love for Carter pushed her back into her car and onto the highway. It pushed her all the way to Bonne Terre.

CARTER LAY ON HIS MOTHER'S bed in the crappy hotel room she'd rented off the highway. Some of her clothes were there, a raincoat, a turtleneck. Cold weather clothes, left behind. Like him.

Why am I here? he thought, staring at the same cracks on the ceiling that he'd been staring at for five days. Today was his last day. Vanessa had paid out the week and that was it.

Five days waiting here and he knew what he'd known when he'd first arrived.

There would be no satisfaction from his mother. No explanations. No tearful apologies.

She'd left, taken her thirty silver coins, and she wasn't coming back. But this time, she had to know that if she came back, he'd send her to the cops.

The rage billowed in him, but he'd already destroyed the lamp, broken the mirror. The TV would never work again. His cell phone was trashed.

There was nothing left for him to throw. Nothing left to keep him here.

It was over. Done. The secret was out and there was no more protecting anyone. All those secrets and lies, the distance he put between himself and anything he wanted to keep clean—it was all over.

The shell was gone and his skin flinched in the cool air.

But still he couldn't walk out that yellowed door.

What do I have to go back to? he wondered. What did he want to go back to?

Before he'd smashed his phone there had been a dozen calls from Eric Lafayette, messages offering him a job—but Carter couldn't work up the enthusiasm.

Zoe?

His heart spasmed fresh hurt. Fresh pain.

He missed her. He missed her more than his job. His condo. His life. He missed her like he missed his family. Like he missed being touched and loved. He missed her like he missed himself—the man he was without the secrets.

But what could he possibly say that would erase what he'd done? The words he'd used to slice her into pieces?

He cringed and sat up, hanging his head in his hands. This suddenly felt so familiar. This place—not the room or the cracks on the ceiling—but this place in his head.

Giving up something he wanted. Something he loved, because it was easier not to fight. Easier to numb the pain and let the distance take over.

His mother had put him in this place again, left him here all by himself, and he had the same choice to make.

Love or no love.

Alone or with someone. With a family.

When he thought about it like that, it seemed so clear.

"Oh God," he muttered, scrubbing at his face. "I'm so stupid."

His hands ached to touch Zoe. His arms hurt without her in them.

He stood, opened the yellowed door.

"Goodbye, Mom," he breathed and shut the door behind him.

THE LIGHTS WERE ON in Zoe's loft and his stomach dropped into his shoes. She was going to be so mad, he thought. Hurt. Maybe badly enough that she'd never forgive him.

And she was right, he thought, remembering what he'd said to her, like she meant nothing to him.

But he had to try.

He looked down at his wrinkled clothes. No doubt he smelled bad. He'd been living on fast food and beer for a week.

But somehow, the man under the smell was worse. He had no job, no career, and his mother had sold him out for what looked like a plane ticket to South America.

Even if Zoe wasn't so mad she never wanted to see him again, it's not as if he was bringing her his best game. The best version of himself. He didn't even have flowers. What was some abject groveling without flowers?

He should go home. At least shower off the stink.

But God, every minute now felt like a year and

he was all too aware of every second he'd wasted already.

"You going to stand out there all night?" a woman asked from the open doorway.

"No," he said, and stepped toward the concrete step and safety glass door where he'd first tried to kiss Zoe. A Christmas elf was stuck to the door. Mocking him. "Thank you. I'm looking for Zo—"

It was Penny standing there, holding open the door like she expected him.

"Took you long enough," she said, her lips a firm line. "If you didn't surface here or at your condo tonight, I was under strict rules to call the cops."

"I've been..." A hundred lies came to his lips, but he didn't have the energy to build a new house of cards. "Scared."

"You should be," she said. "You hurt that girl pretty bad."

His stomach flopped around like a dying fish and there was nothing he could say.

"This is a mistake, isn't it?" he asked her, naked and vulnerable in a way he'd never been before.

Penny took a deep breath. "No," she finally said. "Zoe's tough, and once she loves you, well..." Now Penny looked chagrined, as if remembering all the hurtful things she'd said. "It takes a lot to change her mind. And frankly, once you love that girl— you're hers. Forever."

That's what it felt like. Like she'd sewn her name on his collar and no matter where he got lost, he'd always find his way back to her.

Hope was a very weak candle in his chest.

"I'd like to speak to her," he said, stepping up on the cement step.

"She's not here."

"Where is she?" he asked, suddenly panicked.

"She said she was going to wait for you," she said. "Where she knew you'd turn up eventually."

IF CARTER HAD FELT ROUGH at Zoe's, after a five-hour drive in the middle of the night he felt like week-old roadkill. But that glimmer of hope that Penny had ignited in his chest had become a fire of purpose.

He arrived at Bonne Terre at dawn, ready to storm any gate that stood in his way. The red front door wasn't locked, and he stepped into The Manor and felt as though he'd been sucked back in time. A kid again, walking through these doors for the first time. Alone. Scared. But determined to keep his family together.

What he wasn't expecting was his grand-mother.

"Well, well," Margot said, sitting in a fresh pool of new sunlight in the kitchen. She looked some-how both old and young at dawn, as if the years behind her were long but not nearly as interesting, in her estimation, as the years to come. Her sleek white hair was loose around her face, and her blue eyes were as sharp as hooks. "Look what the cat dragged in."

"Is Zoe here?"

"She is. But she's sleeping," she said, her voice sharp when he started up the stairs to find her. "And that woman needs her sleep, Carter. She's upset and pregnant."

Guilt body slammed him, and he stepped back into the kitchen and collapsed into an empty seat at the table.

She stared at him over her teacup as if she was the queen and he was less than nothing. "You've been busy."

He didn't know what to say to that so he was silent, playing with the homemade jingle bell centerpiece in the middle of the table.

"Vanessa?"

"Gone," he said. "For good. South America maybe. She's got people after her for money. The gems…" He paused, tired of the words before they even came out of his mouth. Tired of his life.

"She thought the gems would get her out of a jam. Get her out of the life."

"Those damn gems," Margot said, her voice burning, and his gaze flickered to hers. "Caused us more trouble than they're worth."

"Uncle Carter?" Carter spun to see a sleepy, wild-haired Katie on the steps.

"Hiya, Katie," he said, standing as she leaped off the steps into his arms.

"We've been so worried!" she cried. "Mom is totally freaking out and Uncle Tyler is pretending like nothing's the matter but he and Aunt Juliette are thinking about hiring a private eye and Zoe is—"

There was a thump and a patter of feet on the floors above them and within moments Zoe was on the steps. His chest collapsed at the sight of her. She was so pale. Big black circles lined her eyes, and the swell of her belly against a long white nightgown seemed to dwarf her.

Margot pulled Katie out of his arms, and he stared, blind and dumb, at the woman he'd hurt.

"I'm so sorry," he breathed.

She was dry-eyed, but her hand trembled against the banister as she stepped down into the kitchen. "For scaring us?" she said. "Or for being so cruel before you left?"

"For both," he breathed. "For everything."

He became dimly aware that his whole family was filtering into the kitchen. Savannah and her husband, Matt. Tyler and his wife, Juliette. His whole life, everything he'd denied and turned away, left behind in an effort to protect, was right here, right at the worst and best moment of his life.

But not for a moment did he take his eyes off Zoe.

"Are you okay?" she asked, her little chin lifted, and he wondered if she'd been taking royalty lessons from Margot. He nodded because his throat was so clogged with words. All the things he wanted to say to everyone in the room were suddenly desperate for freedom.

My family, he thought. *This is my whole family.*

"Where have you been?" she asked.

He wanted to tell her that it didn't matter, wanted to spare her the seediness of his last five days, but he looked over at his brother. His sister. Their blond hair like halos in the morning light. He saw them as they were and as they had been as children, and he knew he wasn't that different from Zoe's mother. They watched him with knowing eyes—Tyler's in particular seemed to be telling him not to be an idiot anymore.

And he knew for the rest of his life he wouldn't spare anyone anything.

It hurt too much. Cost too much.

"I've spent the last week in Mom's hotel room," he said, and just about everyone's mouth fell open. "Thinking she might show up and tell me it was all just a big mistake. But she's gone. Without the money from the jewels she thought we had…I think she had to leave the country."

Margot stood, her chair raking across the hardwood and then she left out the back door. He wondered what pain Margot had suffered over Vanessa, but he had more important things to worry about than the past.

He had his future on the line.

"It was her," Carter said to Zoe. "She gave the information to Blackwell. I knew it all along. Those things I said to you…I'm so sorry." His voice cracked, and he couldn't believe it but he was about to cry. Tyler was never going to let go of this, but Carter couldn't stop it. Couldn't control it.

"I was scared," he said. "My whole life I've been scared. Of being hurt again like I was when my mom abandoned us. I froze you out because my life was falling apart and I was terrified. I still am. I have no job, Zoe. No career. Nothing but a bad reputation, but none of it matters. Nothing matters…but you. Your mom said—"

"You saw my mom?" she asked.

"She sent me here, sort of," he said. "But she said once someone loves you, they're yours. And it's true, Zoe. I'm yours, whether you want me or not. You told me that you were falling in love with me and I need to tell you that I am in love with you. I've been in love with you since the moment you stood on that chair."

"Carter—" She sighed, but it wasn't happy. "So much has happened to you. Is this some sort of…I don't know…?"

"Act of desperation," Tyler filled in. The ass.

"Could we get some privacy?" Carter snapped, and his family started to clear the room.

"I'm glad you're back," Savannah whispered before giving him a quick hug. Tyler patted his back.

"Try not to blow this," Tyler said. "We like her."

Finally the room was empty of O'Neills and he was alone with Zoe.

"I think your brother is right—this might be an act of desperation," Zoe said.

"I know." Carter laughed and it felt so good he did it some more. Why did this feel so good? Maybe it was the ten cups of coffee, or maybe it was finally living a life without control. "I'm totally desperate. I'm an absolute mess, and I wouldn't blame you if you didn't want to have anything to do with me. But I have to say, Zoe, I feel better than I have in years. I've spent my whole life frightened, trying to control everything. And I don't have to do that anymore. All I have to do is love you. And I do."

Zoe stared at him, level and calm, unmoved by

his words. It made him feel desperate, lost, and he realized that this was how he'd made her feel. He'd shut her out like this when she'd been naked in front of him.

His instinct was to pull back, save himself, protect himself somehow, but he couldn't. She'd been so brave, loving him. Showing him every scar and ugly place in her life. The least he could do was show her every beautiful thing he saw when he looked at her.

"You're the most uncontrollable force of nature I've ever met. You're unpredictable, and unorthodox. You wear your whole heart on the outside of your body and aren't happy unless I'm doing the same. You make me laugh and you make me feel good. And this baby...your baby...is a product of your bravery and that gigantic heart that I admire and respect so much."

She blinked, her eyes damp, and his heart soared in relief. "I know I don't have much to offer you. I mean, in terms of security. Eric has offered me some kind of job, but I don't know what that is. I might be on a road crew, which I hear makes good money, so you wouldn't have to worry about that. But—" He was babbling, like Zoe when she was nervous, and it wasn't until she laughed that he could stop talking.

"I don't care about your money," she said. "All I've ever cared about is you."

He sighed with pleasure, her words like a warm bath he could ease into. "I know I'm late to the game," he whispered, carefully reaching out for her belly, that taut swell of hope and excitement and love waiting to be born. "But I swear I will spend the rest of my life caring about you and this child."

Her breath shuddered and hiccuped and then she was crying and in his arms and he couldn't hold her close enough.

"She's crying!" Katie cried through the door, the little spy. "But they're hugging so I think it's good."

"I'm so sorry," he whispered into her hair, against her skin. "I will never hurt you like that again. I love you so much."

He heard Savannah cheer in the other room and he groaned. "At least you've met my family," he said. "They can't scare you away now."

"I love your family," she said, cupping his cheeks and kissing his lips. "Almost as much as I love you."

"Christ, Carter, can we come in?" Tyler yelled through the door. "It's like a weeping pregnant women's club out here."

"Come in!" Zoe cried, tipping back her head and laughing. The full-throated sound made him drunk with love. With affection. For everyone.

Then his family was there, their arms around

them both, their love and laughter ringing through his ears. His life. The years away from them had dried out parts of his body, and they were suddenly flush and living again, tingling and painful like flesh waking up.

So much joy.

"Here's what's left of the goddamned gems!" Margot cried, and everyone turned to watch her plunk a potted orchid on the kitchen table.

CHAPTER NINETEEN

MARGOT GRABBED THE ORCHID at the base of the plant and yanked it from its pot. Its fleshy roots dripped dirt like blood.

Carter shared a wild look with Savannah and Tyler.

"This was supposed to end it," Margot said. "Get her out of our lives for good. Stop the damned bleeding of money from this family." She tossed the orchid on the table and from inside the pot dug out a black bag wrapped in tape.

Casual, like it was a baseball, she tossed it to Carter.

"Consider it a wedding gift."

"What the hell?" he breathed, his fingers ripping at the duct tape.

Within seconds the blood-red glitter of a ruby peeked out of the black plastic.

"You've got to be kidding me," Tyler laughed, plucking the palm-sized gem from the bag. He held its crimson brilliance up to the light. "It was in the greenhouse? All this time?"

"Margot had it all along," Savannah said, and

slumped into a chair. "You lied to me." Her husband, Matt, stroked her hair.

"Margot," Carter said through clenched teeth, "you have a lot of explaining to do."

Margot sat down at the table, all her earlier queenly elegance gone. "I'd been keeping tabs on Vanessa and your father for a long time, making sure they wouldn't come back into our lives. And, I won't lie to you—"

"You say that now," Tyler said, bristling with anger. "But clearly, you've been lying to us for years."

Carter couldn't muster up much anger, or frankly, much surprise. Maybe he was just too tired. Or maybe he wasn't surprised by his family anymore. He wrapped his arms around Zoe, wondering how much worse this was going to get.

"I won't apologize," Margot said, her cheeks red and her eyes flashing.

"My father spent seven years in jail," Matt said. "You owe someone some apologies."

The fire banked in Margot's eyes, and a lifetime of regrets, anger, desperation, all poured out of his grandmother.

"After I heard about Vanessa approaching you in that breaking and entering case," Margot said, looking at Carter, "I realized that no amount of money was going to keep her away. So I waited for the perfect chance to get rid of her. Three years later I heard that Richard had been approached about the casino job. It didn't take much to leak some information to Vanessa, who I knew wouldn't be able to resist being at the drop-off site, hoping to get in on the action. The plan was to have both of them arrested and out of our hair for a long time."

"Instead, Dad vanished, Mom vanished, and Matt's dad was arrested," Savannah cried.

"That wasn't my fault," Margot said. "All I did was give Vanessa the information she needed to be there, and I knew she would take care of the rest. Once Richard saw Vanessa, he left—"

"Were you there?" Carter asked.

"Of course," Margot said, and Tyler laughed.

"Of course she was—an eighty-year-old grandmother in a biker bar in Henderson. Makes perfect sense," Tyler breathed.

"I had to be sure it worked, because I knew I wouldn't get a chance like that again."

"Unbelievable," Tyler muttered. "Un-freaking-believable."

"Richard left the jewel case with Joel, Matt's father, but Joel wasn't a thief. He wasn't even a crook. He was just a guy who knew casinos, so Vanessa made an easy mark of him. She managed to get the emerald out of the case, but once she heard the sirens, she slipped it into Joel's pocket and left out the back. In the chaos, I grabbed the case and tried to get the emerald out of Joel's pocket so he wouldn't get in trouble, but there was no time."

"Did you call the cops?" Savannah asked, and Margot nodded.

"I'm sorry, Matt. I am. I didn't mean for your father to get arrested," Margot said.

"I'm so sorry, Matt," Savannah whispered, her hand tugging on the edge of his T-shirt.

Matt stroked his wife's hair, his smile so tender it made Carter glad his sister had found such a man. "Dad knew the risk when he got involved," Matt said.

"Mom broke into the greenhouse," Tyler said. "And I searched this place top to bottom and only found the diamond. What were you doing? Moving the gems around?"

Margot shook her head. "I don't know how Vanessa missed the ruby. When I cleaned up the next morning after the first break-in, I found the bag in the corner, under some broken glass. It was a fluke. Seven years ago, I put the diamond in the attic and the ruby in the greenhouse and I waited. I knew Vanessa would show up eventually, looking for those gems."

"This was a long shot at best," Tyler said. "Your odds—"

"I know," Margot said, and suddenly she looked every one of her years. The sparkle and sizzle of

Carter's grandmother was gone, and now she sat at her kitchen table, an old woman, surrounded by an angry and disbelieving family and piles of regrets. "But she was bleeding me. Paying her every year was going to bankrupt me at some point."

"Why didn't you just give her the gems?" Matt asked.

"She wouldn't have stayed away," Carter answered. "Margot could have given her the gems, but Vanessa would have been back for another ten grand in a few years. She's a bottomless hole."

"And I wanted her to get caught," Margot snapped. "I wanted her far away from us."

"This is nuts, Margot!" Tyler snapped.

"You lied!" Savannah cried. "I asked you if the gems were here and you said no. We could have helped you. We could have figured something out."

"I understand what you did," Carter said, and everyone turned to face him. "The risks you took to keep your family safe."

Margot nodded. "It wasn't an easy decision, but when you gave her that alibi and I knew it was a lie—that she had blackmailed you into it. And I knew she would just keep coming at us. It was only a matter of time before she destroyed our lives. I'm sorry, Carter," she breathed, her broken heart in her eyes. "I was too late to help you."

He nodded and leaned his head against Zoe's.

"She's gone," he said, thinking of that lonely hotel room and those broken fingers. "She can't come back—people far more scary than us are looking for her."

The room was silent, everyone trying to make sense of the eighty-year-old criminal mastermind who was also their grandmother.

"I don't know about anyone else, but I need some coffee," Juliette said.

"And some eggs," Savannah said, standing up to go to the stove, her pregnancy leading the way. "Zoe? You want some? You should eat."

Zoe agreed, and suddenly, everyone was just going on about their day.

Coffee. Eggs.

A giant stolen ruby in the middle of the table.

Laughter, slightly hysterical but totally unstoppable, burped out of Carter. He laughed so hard he had to sit down and then, never one to be left out of a good time, Tyler joined in, his hands on Carter's shoulders.

Then Savannah, who had to brace herself against the stove.

This was his family. Love it, hate it; he couldn't change it and didn't want to. He'd take them, all of them, his gem-stealing grandmother, his sparkling devil of a brother, his too-good-for-the-world sister.

He had them now and he was never going to let them go.

Zoe plunked herself down on his lap, smiling into his eyes. "Let me in on the joke," she whispered.

"I think you have to be a Notorious O'Neill to get it," he whispered, and leaned forward to kiss her. "You're pretty notorious, but we need to work on the O'Neill part," he said, rubbing her belly. The baby kicked and he took that as a yes vote.

"Are you asking me to marry you?" Zoe asked, and he nodded.

"A Christmas wedding," he said. "A spring baby. What could be better?"

Zoe sighed and curled up against him, his sunshine on all the dark unknown days ahead. "Nothing," she sighed. "Nothing at all."

EPILOGUE

One Year Later

"WE MAYBE SHOULD HAVE TALKED to each other before everyone decided to have babies," Tyler said, trying to jam a deck of cards into one of the kids' stockings. "We could have scheduled this better."

"Is that the last of it?" Carter asked, checking the floor for any little pony or forgotten doll.

"I think so."

Tyler stepped back next to Carter and they looked at the stockings strung up against the mantel in The Manor's library. The Christmas tree glittered behind them, practically levitating on piles of presents. "It's a lot of pink," Carter said.

"Poor Jake is the odd man out," Tyler said, talking about his son, born five months after Savannah's Faith, who had been born early, six weeks after Amelia. "We need more boys."

"I need more sleep," Carter muttered.

"Amen to that," Tyler said with a smile. The glimmer was turned down on Ty these days—no sleep and dirty diapers could do that to a man. But there was a steadfastness in him that hadn't been there before.

A steadfastness Carter never thought he'd see in his devilish little brother.

"I'm proud of you, Tyler," Carter said, and Tyler blinked. "I don't say that enough. But I mean it. You are a good man."

"Thank you," Tyler said, his voice rough. "That means a lot."

"I should have said it more when we were growing up. I should have done more—"

"Stop, man. We're together now. The three of us. Our kids. That's all that matters."

"Hi, guys," Savannah said, stepping into the room and right into the space between her brothers. "Wow. It looks like Christmas exploded in here."

"What are you doing up?" Carter asked, wrapping an arm around his sister. Savannah liked hugs, and he was making up for lost time.

"Checking on Margot."

"How is she?" Tyler asked.

"Sleeping comfortably."

They were silent, staring into the glitter and gleam of a holiday at the Manor. Maybe Margot's last one. None of them said it, but the thought was there, as much a part of the holiday as the food and gifts. They'd returned the ruby to the casino anonymously last year, and three months later Margot had had a stroke.

And then another.

Carter and Zoe tried to come back to The Manor as often as they could. It was difficult with the baby and Zoe's academy taking off like it was, but everyone was well aware that Margot didn't have much longer to live.

Luckily, the foundation work he did for Lafayette Corp. he could do from anywhere.

"She's had a good life," Tyler said. "She's eighty-five—"

"No, she's not!" Carter said. "She's like seventy."

Savannah laughed. "You're both wrong. Matt and I were looking for her will and we found her birth certificate. Margot's ninety-two."

"Shut. Up," Tyler whispered, and shook his head. "What a woman."

"What a Mom," Savannah said. "Good and bad. We couldn't have had a better one."

"No," Carter agreed. "And I couldn't have a better brother or sister."

Savannah held his hand, and Tyler's arm around his shoulder felt like the best kind of anchor, keeping him here, present and rooted in his life.

"We're starting a new legacy," he said. "For our kids."

Savannah nodded. "Something they can be proud of. Part of Margot, but parts of us."

"And hopefully a good portion of the people we married," Tyler said, and they all nodded. "But I'm still teaching all our kids how to play five-card."

Savannah groaned.

"I'm not kidding," Tyler said.

"I know," she said. "That's what scares me."

Carter's heart was huge in his chest, love like a balloon. But he suddenly needed Zoe and Amelia.

This love was like that. He'd be in the middle of a meeting and he would need them. Need Amelia's sweet babble, or the touch of Zoe's hand on his. The weight of his girls in his arms.

"Good night, guys," he said. "You should get some sleep—it's going to be a short night."

Tyler groaned, and they all went upstairs to their beds.

He opened the door to his old room. The light from the night-light in the hallway fell over Zoe's sleeping face, the baby nestled against her in the middle of the bed.

It was no way to sleep—with a tornado baby in bed with you—but sometimes it was the best thing in the world.

He slid under the covers as quietly as he could, and Amelia sighed in her sleep, rolled over and flung out a hand, connecting with his face.

Zoe's silent laugh shook the covers. "You okay?" she whispered, her green eyes aglow.

Okay? he thought, suddenly overwhelmed. The woman of his dreams was in his bed, the baby of his heart beside him. His family was asleep in the house around him. Every dream he had ever had for his life had been reborn and made better, because of this woman.

"Sweetie," Zoe sighed, reaching forward and catching the tears that fell from his eyes.

He caught her hand and pressed a kiss to it.

Never in his wild imagination had he thought that being a Notorious O'Neill would make him so damn happy.

* * * * *

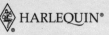

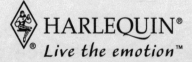

Harlequin® Historical
Historical Romantic Adventure!

Imagine a time of chivalrous knights and unconventional ladies, roguish rakes and impetuous heiresses, rugged cowboys and spirited frontierswomen— these rich and vivid tales will capture your imagination!

Harlequin Historical . . . they're too good to miss!

HARLEQUIN®
Presents®

The world's bestselling romance series...
The series that brings you your favorite authors,
month after month:

Helen Bianchin...Emma Darcy
Lynne Graham...Penny Jordan
Miranda Lee...Sandra Marton
Anne Mather...Carole Mortimer
Melanie Milburne...Michelle Reid

and many more talented authors!

Wealthy, powerful, gorgeous men...
Women who have feelings just like your own...
The stories you love, set in exotic, glamorous locations...

HARLEQUIN®
Presents®

Seduction and Passion Guaranteed!

HPDIR08

www.eHarlequin.com

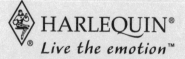